To Bruce
from
Joan, Janet & Jim
Christmas 1964.

Read by
Bruce Byron
Jason + Judy
Summer 1991

THE MYSTERY OF THE
Muffled Man

THE MYSTERY OF

MAX BRAITHWAITE

The Muffled Man

GENERAL EDITOR—ARTHUR HAMMOND

ILLUSTRATED BY J. ROSENTHAL

THE SECRET CIRCLE MYSTERIES NUMBER 5

Little, Brown and Company/Boston, Toronto

Library of Congress Catalog Card No. 62-20655

PRINTED AND BOUND BY
HAZELL WATSON AND VINEY LTD
AYLESBURY AND SLOUGH, ENGLAND

TO
Chris

CONTENTS

1

The Muffled Man Arrives

The night the stranger came to town, Chris Summerville and his pal Dumont LePage stood on the station platform and nearly froze.

Even for this northern mining-town it was cold. Twenty-three below zero. As the boys danced up and down on the platform, newly scraped clean of snow, the wooden planks squeaked with the cold. Even the sign hanging at the end of the station looked cold, and seemed to shiver as it informed the world that this was the town of Canot, population 2,600.

The dog, Arthur, was cold too. He sat on his big bushy tail and looked up at Chris as if to say, "What in heck are we doing out here? This weather's not fit for man or beast!"

But even if he could have said what he thought, nobody would have paid any attention, for it was Arthur's fate in life never to be taken seriously. Not only did his shaggy black-and-white coat give him the look of a friendly Teddy bear, but a white patch on his muzzle, inherited from some unknown ancestor, made it look as if he were always wearing a grin. On top of all that, his master had dubbed him

Arthur, and who can take a dog with a name like that seriously?

Chris, broad-shouldered and a little shorter than his pal Dumont, turned the freezing tip of his nose into the fur of his parka and blew a hot breath to warm it. His mind was miles away from that station platform: on a lake out in the bush and rock of the Canadian Shield. The old trapper and guide, Doodie Horton, had told them about it and, even allowing for Doodie's known lying ability, it sounded good.

"There's still plenty of fish in her," the wrinkled, bent-up old man had said, rubbing his short white beard. "Nobody knows about her, except me and some Cree Indians."

"Will you tell us where it is?" Chris had asked.

"Well, if you promise not to tell anybody else." He looked from one boy to the other sharply. They nodded their heads solemnly.

"Well, she's about four miles northeast of town: little bit of a lake sort of hidden between the big lakes, but packed full of fish. Funny durned thing about them fish," Doodie had gone on. "They seem to bite better in winter than in summer. There's whitefish, pickerel, all kinds: but you've got to have the right bait. Not many knows how to make it."

"How?" Dumont had asked.

"You come round here the day afore you're going fishing and I'll show you," the old man had promised. "Tell you how to find the lake, too. You'll catch more fish'n you can tote home."

And so they had decided to go the day after tomorrow. That is, they'd decided until Chris's mother had dropped the little bombshell that blew their plans to pieces. Chris grimaced with disgust. "A dame!" he said out loud.

Dumont lifted his head out of his high collar. "Eh? Oh, the cousin. *Mon ami,* what does this girl from the city look like?" he asked, purposely making his French-Canadian accent very heavy. As well as being taller than Chris, he was thinner, sharp-faced and nearly always smiling.

"How should I know?" Chris growled back. "I've never seen her."

"I got it!" Dumont slapped his knee. "We go home and tell your mother we couldn't find her."

"Sure! Great idea! And what happens to Carol when she doesn't find anybody here to meet her?"

"She thinks we've all been massacred by the Indians and gets back on the train. City people always think this country is full of Indians."

"And you're full of prunes," Chris said. "If you must get ideas, get a good one for a change."

"Well, we could tell her the woods are full of wolves and then she won't want to go ice-fishing with us."

"So? And then Mum won't let me go, either. Try again."

Dumont pushed his red-and-white toque to the back of his head and thought, but nothing came.

Chris thought, too, back to that same morning when his mother had interrupted Dumont and him in the midst of putting dubbin on their high moccasins.

"I've just had a phone call from your Aunt Janice in the city," she said. "She and Uncle Herbert are going to Bermuda for the Christmas holidays. Isn't that nice?"

Chris agreed that it probably was for them, but decided that personally he'd rather stay right here in Canot where there were some really interesting things to do.

"And you'll never guess what else she told me."

Chris agreed that he probably never would.

"Well, I must say, Mighty Hunter, you don't seem very interested."

"Gosh, Mum, why should I be? If Aunt Janice and Uncle Herbert want to go to Bermuda and lie around in the sun, that's their business."

"And the fact that Carol is coming to stay with us is your business."

"What? Oh no, Mum. She can't!"

"Carol?" Dumont raised his head and grinned. "Who is this Carol who is coming for Christmas? Christmas Carol maybe?"

Chris took a swing at him and missed. "She's a dame from the city."

His mother frowned. "Chris, that's not a very nice way to talk about your cousin." Then she turned to Dumont. "She's a very nice girl, just your age, and a good sport, too."

"But Mum," Chris protested desperately. "Dumont and I have got plans." He wiped the blond hair off his forehead. "She'll just completely ruin everything!"

"What kind of plans?" Mrs Summerville wanted to know.

"Well we're sort of going . . . uh, ice-fishing?" Chris finished pleadingly.

"Oh? Where?"

"On a lake."

"What lake?"

Chris squirmed. "Oh just a small lake a little way from here." Then he added eagerly, "Doodie says it's loaded with fish."

Mrs Summerville smiled at the two boys, who had suddenly become very interested in their moccasins. "Well, I suppose I have no objection to your going ice-fishing, as long as it's close to town. . . ."

"Swell, Mum," Chris said quickly. "Carol can help you or . . ."

". . . and provided you take Carol with you," Mrs Summerville finished.

"What?" It was an explosion from two sources.

"A female girl going ice-fishing with us?" Dumont pointed at himself. "How could this be?"

"Quite simple," Mrs Summerville said. "That is, if she wants to go. Of course, she may prefer skating or skiing, and I'm sure you'll be happy to go with her. And what's more, you'll have to meet the train, Chris. As you know, your father and I absolutely must go to the Board of Trade dinner tonight, and since your father is the president, we can't be late. So you will represent the family."

"But won't she have suitcases and things?"

"Yes, and Hank Osborne always meets the train with his taxi. I'll give you the money for it."

And that is how they came to be standing on the platform waiting for the 8:05 train from the south, and freezing.

Dumont ran over and peeked through the frosty window at the large clock in the waiting-room. "Seven minutes after eight," he announced with a straight face. "Train's due at eight-o-five. Guess it's not coming. Let's go home."

"Wish we could," Chris started to say, and then, as if to contradict Dumont, the diesel engine whistled at the block a half-mile down the track, and the glaring headlight cast eerie shadows on the rails as the engine rounded the bend.

The train, with icicles hanging from it like fringes on a skirt, grated to a stop, and the trainman, bundled up to the eyebrows, climbed down the steps of the first car.

It was then that Chris and Dumont got their first glimpse of the muffled man, right behind the trainman. He was dressed in a long, shabby black overcoat with a fur collar pulled up to his ears, and had a long grey muffler wound round the collar and across his face, hiding all but the eyes. Underneath this Chris thought he made out the white of a bandage. On the man's head was an odd, scruffy cap pulled low on the forehead, almost meeting the scarf.

His feet were covered with a pair of huge buckled overshoes which came up to the bottom of his coat.

To add to his weird appearance, his left sleeve was completely empty and was tucked into the overcoat pocket. In his right hand he carried a thick, knob-handled cane.

Several things happened almost at once.

Arthur, who seemed to consider it his duty to welcome all strangers with a friendly sniff and a tail wag, left Chris's side and bounded towards the stranger.

Chris, who sensed that this was not a friendly type shouted, "No, Arthur! Back, boy!"

Arthur half turned, then gave a friendly "Woof" and bounded on.

The stranger drew back with a snarl of rage, as if he were being attacked by a pack of wolves. He raised his stick above his head and, to Chris's horror, brought it down with all his strength towards Arthur's skull.

Luckily Arthur was quicker than he looked. Sensing the danger, he put on the brakes and, as he skidded forwards on the icy platform, twisted his body frantically to the side, losing his balance as he did so. The stick missed the skull, which it surely would have cracked, and hit the big dog a glancing blow on the ribs.

Arthur let out a howl of pain and retreated towards his master, who sprang indignantly at the stranger. But at that moment the station door opened, and Jim Hall, the station agent, stepped directly in Chris's path. As they collided, the startled Hall grabbed him desperately to prevent them both from falling.

"Here now, what's going on?" the station agent gasped.

"My dog!" Chris sputtered. "That man!"

"Is that mutt of yours causing trouble again?" the agent demanded. "How many times have I told you not to bring him down here! He's a nuisance."

"We know, we know!" Dumont protested, coming up. "But that's no reason for that guy to half kill him. Arthur was only trying to be friendly."

"Oh it's you," Mr Hall said resignedly. "I might have known. Now what are you two kids talking about?"

"That man!" Chris pointed past the station agent towards a pretty girl dressed in a sky-blue jacket, with cap to match, and carrying two very new and expensive suitcases.

"He's gone!" Chris stammered. "Where did he go?"

"You've got to stop him!" Dumont added excitedly. "He looks like some kind of a maniac!"

Jim Hall was slowly losing his mind. "What in the name of old Harry are you kids talking about?"

"The man, the man!" Chris shouted. He almost added "you dope," but remembered in time that that was no way to talk to an adult.

"There's no man: just this young lady."

The girl in the blue jacket came towards them and put her cases down. "I'm Carol Fitzpatrick. I'm looking for Mr and Mrs Summerville," she said to the station agent.

Jim Hall looked at her and smiled, as if relieved to find some sanity in an otherwise crazy world. "Well, you've come to the right place, young lady, because this confused curmudgeon here is none other than Chris Summerville."

"Chris!" Carol Fitzpatrick exclaimed with obvious delight. "Oh, I'm so glad to meet you. I've heard so much about you."

Chris felt like a fool. He'd been determined that this city cousin wouldn't make him act like a country bumpkin, and now that very thing was happening. "Uh . . . hullo . . ." he stammered, taking her outstretched hand and trying to peer past her to where the stranger had stood. There was nothing there but the dimly lit empty platform.

"Who is your friend?" Carol asked, gaining confidence with Chris's obvious confusion.

"Uh . . . this is Dumont. Did you see where he went?"

"Why, he's right here. How do you do, Dumont?"

"I don't mean him. I mean the man who got off the train. The man in the long coat who was hiding his face."

The girl looked at him and hesitated. "I didn't really notice," she said. "Out through the station, I guess."

Jim Hall snorted, rubbed his ear with his hand, and stepped back into the station waiting-room.

"Let's see where he's heading," Dumont said. "I wouldn't be surprised if he took our taxi! Come on!"

The two boys rushed to the corner of the building, but their taxi was still there. They looked towards the main street of the town. A few people were hurrying along in the cold, but there was absolutely no sign of the man in the long, shabby coat.

Chris called Arthur over to him to see if he was hurt, but the big dog was only shaken up. "Boy, is he mad!" Chris said. "I've never seen his hackles up like that. I wouldn't want to be that guy when Arthur sees him again!"

They went back to where Carol was waiting, holding her hands against her ears to keep out the cold.

"Come on," Chris mumbled. "Mum and Dad couldn't come to meet you because of a big banquet. We'll take a taxi home." He picked up the two suitcases, while Dumont took the skis and poles that the conductor had handed down and left on the station platform.

Hank Osborne had the car running to keep it warm, and it wasn't long before they drove up to the Summerville's large white house at the edge of town.

"What a dream of a house!" Carol exclaimed as they got out of the car. "And look at that snow! I've never seen such high banks. And so white!"

"We usually have black snow," Dumont said, with a grin, as he took the skis from Hank, "but this year we thought we'd like a change."

Carol's laugh rang out on the clear night. "This is going to be more fun than I thought," she said.

Dumont bowed low and motioned with a sweep of his arm for her to follow Chris up the front walk between the six-foot-high banks of snow.

In the front hall Chris was still puzzled. "I wonder where that guy could have gone," he said.

"He went round the end of the station like a frightened buffalo and into a phone booth there," Carol said.

"The phone booth! Then you did notice!" Dumont said, in amazement.

"Of course I did. I saw him in the phone booth as we drove away in the taxi. But I didn't want to say anything to you and have you go picking a fight with him."

"Why not?"

"Because," Carol said, lowering her voice a little, "that man was a very peculiar character indeed. In fact, he was quite frightening. Wait until I tell you what happened on the train!"

2

The Tell-Tale Reflection

"Well, what did happen?" Chris said after a moment, as they hung their coats up in the hall. Carol said nothing, deliberately teasing them, as she began to peek into the various downstairs rooms of the house.

"What happened?" Dumont echoed.

With annoying casualness Carol wandered into the dining-room, the two boys behind her. "Such a pretty house," she said. "And so big. I had no idea."

Dumont gave Chris a look that summed up both their feelings: girls! "You expected maybe an igloo, so far north like?" he said disgustedly.

Carol laughed. "I don't know if I did or not, never having been north before. I know I most definitely didn't expect to be met at the station by a taxi!"

"A dog team, maybe?" Chris asked. "There aren't many of them around this area now. Even some of the hunters and trappers use snowmobiles."

"Except old Arthur," Dumont added. "He's a kind of one-dog team, when we can persuade him to pull the toboggan, that is."

"That sounds like fun!" Carol exclaimed. "I'm so looking forward to skiing and skating and tramping through the woods. Don't tell me the woods are all gone, too."

"Nope, plenty of woods," Chris said. "Matter of fact, they begin practically at the back door. And there are plenty of deer and moose and bear and wolves in 'em, too. Wolves are a blamed nuisance: they kill off the deer and spoil the hunting."

Carol made a face. "You can't scare me. I love it in the woods!"

"Go very far in that bush and you'd be lost for sure," Chris said.

"If I were you, I'd keep out of those woods." Dumont threw a broad wink at Chris.

If Carol noticed the wink, she chose to ignore it. "But what do people do up here?" she said. "I mean for a living? Don't tell me they all hunt and trap."

"Oh no, there's a few explorers searching for the Northwest Passage, and a few wild Indian tribes . . ." Dumont began, but Chris cut him off.

"They work in the gold mine. My dad's a mining engineer there. It's one of the biggest in North America. Then there's a pulp-and-paper mill. It's a big one, too: on the river bank. And some of the men fish. Now, will you please tell us what you were going to say about the muffled man!" Then, because he realized he'd sounded pretty rough, he added, "Please!"

"All right!" Carol sat down at the table, with the boys opposite her. "I noticed him first when he got on the train at Barrie. Well, after all, how could you miss him with that kookie getup: bandages on his face, and a broken arm and all?"

"So that's why his sleeve was empty," Chris said.

"Yes. His arm was in a sling, at least some of the time."

"What do you mean, some of the time?" Chris said.

"Wait a minute," Carol said. "I'm getting ahead of my story. He was in the double seat right across the aisle from me, and I felt kind of sorry for him at first, especially when he had so much trouble with the map and all."

"This kid sure tells a straightforward story," Dumont said with a groan. "What map?"

"I couldn't see it, not just then. But he kept opening it up, spreading it out and studying it. And he had this little crumpled piece of brown paper that he kept looking at, as if he were comparing it with the map. That's not easy with one hand."

"You said something about him using his bad arm," Dumont said.

"That happened after it got dark. I was looking out the window: you know how you can't see anything outside but you can see the reflection of the other people in the coach?"

"Yes."

"Well, he was studying this map again, and it slipped. He reached his left arm right out of the sling to grab it!"

Even Dumont was impressed. "You mean he's a phoney?"

"Did he notice you'd seen him?" Chris said.

"No, because I was looking the other way, at his reflection in the window. But he looked round to make sure nobody had noticed."

"That's sure funny," Chris mused. "I wonder why a guy would pretend to have a broken arm."

"Wait till you hear the rest. Shortly after that two Mounties got on the train. They were just passengers, looking for a seat. Well, you should have seen Old

Mufflers. If ever a man tried to hide in a seat he did. Then he gathered up his things and got up. His map slipped onto the floor and I reached down to help him. Well, you should have heard him!"

"How do you mean?" Chris asked.

"He hissed at me." Carol shuddered. "Like a snake. 'Leave it alone!' he said, and I never heard so much evil in a man's voice."

Dumont started to say something, but the look on Carol's face stopped him. For a second she turned pale, but then she regained her carefree smile.

"Did the Mounties see him?" Chris asked.

"I don't think so. They were just looking for a seat. Anyway, he got out of that coach just as fast as any man ever got out of anywhere and finally the Mounties sat down in his empty seat."

"And you told them the whole story," Dumont prompted.

"How could I? After all, what was there to tell? That the man's voice frightened me, or that I thought I saw him use a broken arm? After all, I only saw the reflection."

Chris was thinking. "That map he was looking at, what was it like?"

Carol thought. "Well, I don't know. I don't know anything about maps. But it was a big square thing, with all sorts of marks on it. They looked like lakes and rivers, and a lot of squiggly lines."

Without speaking, Chris got up and left the room. They heard him go into a room across the hall. In a moment he was back with a large square map. "Like this one?" he asked, spreading it out on the table.

"That's it," Carol gasped. "The very one. Or, at least,

it looks like it. I remember that pink spot there with the white lines across it."

"That pink spot, as you call it, is the great and important town of Canot," Dumont said.

"Then the map he was looking at . . ." Carol began.

". . . was the Department of Lands and Forests map of this area," Chris finished. "They put them out for every area in the province. It shows just about everything there is to show."

Carol was studying the map. "Just look at all the lakes, would you!" she said. "It must be wonderful in the summer."

"The most important lake of the lot isn't even on the map," Dumont said. "Or, at least, it doesn't have a name."

"Oh?" Carol's eyes were round. "What lake's that?"

"Just the best lake in the world for ice-fishing," Dumont said.

"Ice-fishing?"

"Yeah." Chris was frowning thoughtfully. "I wonder why that guy was studying a map of this area so carefully," he said. "I wonder . . . I wonder."

"Why not?" Dumont said. "He was getting off the train here."

"I think I know." Carol's smile was as pleased as a smile can be. "Wait until I show you the most important piece of evidence of all. It's in my jacket pocket."

She got up from her chair and started towards the hall closet. But she didn't get there. Suddenly, Arthur shattered the air with a bark and nearly knocked her over as he headed for the front door.

The door opened and Mrs Summerville burst in and gathered Carol in her arms. "Oh, it's good to see you! And haven't you grown? Did you have a good trip?" she cried, along with all the other things that fond aunts say to nieces.

And Carol, who was really fond of her Aunt Mary, squealed and gurgled her happiness in the same way.

Alec Summerville, a tall, lean man with sandy hair, stood by with a pleased smile on his face until he could get a word in. Then he shook hands with Carol. "Well, we certainly are glad to have you with us," he said. "I hope you won't find it too dull up here in the north woods."

"Good heavens, no!" Carol said, looking at Chris and Dumont. "If it keeps up anything like it's begun, it'll be the most exciting week of my life."

"Wonderful!" Mrs Summerville said, beaming at her son. "Then the boys have told you about their ice-fishing trip?"

"Ice-fishing! Oh that sounds simply wonderful!"

The boys looked at each other and shrugged.

"How do you do it?" Carol went on.

Dumont groaned. "Well, it's pretty simple. You just go where there's plenty of ice, and fish for it. You use snow-flakes for bait."

"Dumont!" Mrs Summerville's tone was warning.

"No, it means fishing through the ice," Chris explained. "You chop a hole in a lake and put down a line."

"But isn't it terribly cold?" Carol asked.

"Yeah, but most people have little huts, with stoves in them, and this little hole in the ice is inside the hut. It's good fun," he added. He realized that now that he knew her he didn't mind the idea of Carol going with them, after all.

"It'll be a pretty long hike getting there," Dumont added. "And the snow's two feet deep." But he was only pretending not to want her: he felt all right about Carol going now, too.

"Poof!" Carol scoffed. "Who's afraid of snow? This is going to be fun!"

Chris looked at his mother as though he knew what her next remark would be, and he was right. "But is it safe?" she asked, looking at her husband with a worried frown.

"If they're careful," Alec Summerville said. "Tim Beaton's got a hut out on Gander Lake. He said they could use it any time they wanted to. It's only about half a mile out of town. Tim will probably be out there himself, to keep an eye on them."

Chris started to say that they were planning to go to Doodie's special lake. Then he remembered promising not to mention it to anybody. As he sat puzzling over this, his mother asked him to go and get some wood for the fireplace, while she got cake and ice cream from the kitchen. Carol went with her and Mr Summerville went into his study for a few minutes. Then, in the excitement of the rest of the evening, as Carol and his parents exchanged news and gossip about the various members of the family, Chris forgot all about his problem of the lake.

That night, after Dumont had finally had enough cake and ice cream and had gone home and all the news had been exchanged, Chris lay awake in his room, with Arthur stretched out on the rug beside the bed.

The problem of who the strange muffled man could be and of why he had acted so mysteriously on the train kept running through his head. The fact that he had been so frightened of the Mounties sounded ominous, all right.

His mind wouldn't rest. There was something trying to

get into it, something Carol had said: no, something Carol had been going to show them. Yes, that was it: just before his parents had come in. She'd been going to show them something. What was it? He'd have to remember to ask her first thing in the morning.

He went to sleep and dreamed that he was unwinding the muffler from the face of the muffled man. And when he got it off, there was no face there at all: just a big hole.

3

The Brown-Paper Map

But it wasn't until some time after breakfast the next morning that Chris did remember to ask Carol what it was she had been going to show them.

He and Dumont were showing Carol around the house and had reached the basement workshop.

"This is where Dad tests samples for some of the prospectors around," Chris said, pulling open a drawer full of jagged pieces of various kinds of rocks.

"What does your father do in the mine?" Carol said.

"He's the chief assayer."

"What's that?"

"He tests samples of ore from the mine to find out how much gold there is in them. If the ore's rich enough they bring it up to the surface and refine it."

"Golly! I'd sure like to go into the mine some time. Do you suppose I could?" Carol asked.

"Sure," Chris said. "Dad can arrange it for us."

"And maybe we can do a little plain and fancy highgrading," Dumont added.

"What's that?" Carol said.

"Stealing highgrade ore from the mine," Chris explained.

"Some of the ore has so much gold in it that a miner can take ten or even twenty dollars' worth out in his pockets, if he doesn't get caught. Some of them sometimes try it."

"But what could he do with the ore? I mean, it isn't something you can just walk into a store with, is it?"

"There are people who buy it," Chris said. "Crooks. They travel around and collect it from all the people who steal it from the mines. Then they send it to Montreal or some place like that to be refined. It's a sort of syndicate."

Carol jumped down off the stool she'd been perched on. "That's it!" she said. "The muffled man! He's a highgrader!"

"Naw," Dumont said scornfully.

"He might be a spy of some kind," Chris said quietly. "I've been thinking. You know, there's a rumour that they've discovered uranium in the mine, as well as gold."

"Well I think he's a highgrader, representing this crime syndicate," Carol maintained.

"And I think he's a guy with a cold nose, who likes to keep it muffled up," Dumont scoffed, "and who doesn't like shaggy dogs."

"How can you say that in spite of all the evidence?" Carol said. "The hidden face, the way he was afraid of the police, pretending to have a broken arm?"

"Hey, now I know what I was trying to remember!" Chris exclaimed. "Last night just before Mum and Dad came in, remember? You said something about the most important evidence of all."

Carol's eyes widened. "How dopey can I get! Of course! It's in my jacket pocket." She dashed up the basement steps and in a few seconds was back.

"What do you think of this, Mr Wiseguy?" she said to Dumont, holding out a tattered piece of brown paper, very worn and wrinkled, with faint pencil markings on it.

"Your birth certificate maybe?" Dumont said.

"No, you dope!" she said, waving it triumphantly. "It's the piece of paper the muffled man was comparing with the map! When he got up in such a great hurry, this fell on the floor with the map and he didn't notice it. I found it on the floor after he was gone."

Chris took the crumpled paper and studied the faint markings. "Sure has been handled a lot," he said. "These lines are so faint you can hardly see them."

"What are they anyway?" Dumont asked.

"Some kind of a map or diagram," Carol said.

"Yeah." Chris's forehead was wrinkled. "This here could be the shore of a lake, maybe." He twisted the paper to get more light on it. "Looks to me as if it was drawn in an awful hurry."

"And with a blunt pencil," Dumont added.

"What's that?" Carol asked, pointing to a faint mark on a crease in the paper.

"It looks like an X or something," Chris said, "marking some special place maybe."

"And this funny looking thing?" Dumont pointed. "It looks like a stepladder or something."

"Could be a fire tower, maybe," Chris suggested.

"Do you know if there's a fire tower anywhere near here?" Carol asked.

Chris shook his head. "Nope. But there are probably lots of them in the bush. This is pretty wild country, especially all north of town: just bush, no roads at all. So we don't really know it at all. About the only way to get

around up there is in an aeroplane with floats or skis, to land on one of the lakes."

Carol was thinking hard. "Are there many gold mines in this part of the country?"

"About twenty maybe, inside a distance of about fifteen miles. They're all south of here," Chris told her.

"That's it then!" Carol said excitedly. "Don't you see? Of course it is! This is the place where they pick up the highgrade, whatever it is, from all the mines! Then they fly it out from this other place marked on the lake."

"Could be," Chris said thoughtfully. Then he looked at Carol. "Does this guy know you have this?"

"Well, he'll certainly know that he's lost it, and probably where. And he certainly knows what I look like, because he stared right into my face." Carol made a face at the memory of it.

"Maybe we should give this to the police," Chris suggested.

"I've got a better idea," Dumont said.

"What?"

"Try and give it back to the man who lost it. After all, it must be fairly important to him if he kept looking at it so much, and he's in town. Where could he go? There's no train out until tonight. He's probably staying down at the hotel. You've got no evidence at all that he's really a crook, and this is his property."

"You're crazy!" Chris exploded. "After the way he attacked poor old Arthur?"

"And the way he behaved on the train?" Carol added. "I certainly wouldn't want to be the one to meet up with him again and tell him I had the paper!"

"Well, it makes more sense than going down to the police

station and telling Chief Greenway," Dumont retorted. "I know what he'd say: 'You teenagers are nuts!' "

"Doodie Horton!" Chris said suddenly. "Of course! Why didn't I think of it sooner? If anyone can recognize the things on this map, he can."

"Who in the world is Doodie Horton?" Carol said.

"An old prospector . . ." Chris began.

". . . who looks like Santa Claus in a dirty beard," Dumont went on. "He's been around this country all his life: prospected it, hunted it, trapped it, guided city dudes through it. Why, he knows the bush for miles around as well as I know my own yard."

"We've got to go and see Doodie today anyway," Chris said. "He's going to give us some special bait for ice-fishing and tell us where to find his lake."

"Where does he live?" Carol asked.

"In a little cabin on the edge of town. Yessir, he'll tell us what part of the country this paper is supposed to show!"

Dumont agreed, but just as they were getting up to go and call on old Doodie right away, they heard the telephone ringing upstairs and Mrs Summerville answering it. She called down to say that Dumont was wanted.

Trying to think of what chores he might have left undone at home, Dumont went up to answer it. He was back in two minutes with a puzzled look on his face. "What do you know about that?" he said, thoughtfully.

"Know about what?" Chris asked.

"That was Dad on the phone. He wants me to go down to the hardware store and help him. Says our store was broken into last night and some things stolen!"

"What kind of things?" Chris said.

"Well, a sharp spade, a pick, a thirty-thirty rifle and some ammunition, and. . . ." He paused and stared at Chris and Carol for a moment.

"And what?" they said, almost together.

"Four sticks of dynamite!"

4

Crime Wave

As they dashed out to go with Dumont to his father's store, Carol gave a little cry of surprise and put her hand up to her cheek. "It's cold!" she said. "You can feel it in your nose: sort of tingly!" Her breath showed in the air like smoke as she talked.

Chris looked at the large thermometer on the back porch. "Just, let me see, fifteen below!" he said.

"Shucks, that's not cold, partner," Dumont scoffed. "You should see it when it really gets cold up here. Why, boiling coffee freezes before it hits the cup. Ever seen frozen boiling coffee?"

Carol began to shake her head and then caught on. "Oh stop it! I just meant that it was so nice and warm inside the house that it's hard to realize it's so cold outside." She held her mittened hand against her face as they went along the narrow walk round the house, between the six-foot snowbanks.

Arthur tried to pay attention to everyone at once. He jumped up on Chris and almost bowled him over, changed direction and became tangled in Carol's legs, and then bounded up on the snowbank and barked at nothing.

It was a bright day with no clouds. Everything was covered with snow. Each roof had a topping like whipped cream with long clear icicles hanging down from the eaves. Even the fence posts wore white bonnets of snow.

The smoke from the chimneys hung for a moment in the still air and then, because of the cold air up above, instead of spiralling up, slid down off the side of the roofs.

On one side of the street were attractive new frame houses, painted white or in pastel shades. On the other side was the deep bush.

"Do you know, fifteen years ago there wasn't a sign of a town here," Dumont told Carol as they walked along, their overshoes squeaking on the snow. "Just bush. Then they made the big strike and the company built this town from nothing."

"And when all the gold has been dug out of the mine the town will disappear as fast as it came," Chris said. "But that will be a long time from now, my dad says."

"Why did they give it such a crazy name?" Carol asked. "Canot? Cannot what?"

This really broke Dumont up. "Cannot!" he whooped. "Oh you English! Canot is pronounced Can-oh. It rhymes with snow. It's French for canoe and a canoe is a thing you put in water and..."

"I know! I know what a canoe is!" Carol said quickly, as the two boys laughed.

They crossed a bridge and then went up a hill into the main business street of the town. It was decorated for Christmas, with strings of red and green electric lights criss-crossing over the street from the hydro poles at the sides. At each end of the block a large spruce tree, at least fifty feet high, was decorated with more lights.

As they walked along the sidewalk, separated from the road by another high bank of snow, Carol stopped in front of a store window. "What a darling dress!" she said. "It's as cute as anything I've seen in the city!"

"Women wear 'em up here, too, you know," Dumont quipped. "And high-heeled shoes."

"I just can't get over it," Carol said. "I mean, you're so far north, and out there," she waved her arm towards the north, "it's all wild bush. But here, golly! This could be a shopping-area in the city!"

Neither boy had anything to say to this. To them, there was nothing surprising about it. And now they reached the hardware store, its windows filled with a strange mixture of items: electric coffee percolators and snowshoes, high-powered rifles and fancy glassware.

Dumont banged on the locked front door. His father opened it, and motioned impatiently for them to come in.

Gratien LePage, Dumont's father, was a big, broad-shouldered man with a heavy black moustache. In his day he'd been a pulp-wood cutter, a log-driver on the river, and a hard-rock miner. After he had married, he'd saved his money and started the hardware business.

But, still, every minute that he could spare from the store Gratien LePage spent in the woods, hunting or fishing.

Now Mr LePage was flustered and busy. "So, you finally made it, hey?" he said to his son. His accent was much thicker than Dumont's. Dumont grinned and started to say something, but his father, who was looking at the pile of snowshoes with black, piercing eyes, exclaimed, "Ha, ha! Something else is missing!"

"George!" he bellowed to the back of the store. "Come and see this!"

Chief George Greenway, who had been checking the broken lock on the back door, came towards the front of the store. He was a tall man with hair which had already turned grey, though he was still quite young. His blue serge uniform was carefully pressed. As head of Canot's two-man police force, he was always called "Chief." Since there was little crime in such a small town, he was friends with everybody who lived there.

"Something else?" he asked Gratien LePage.

"Something else for sure. A pair of twenty-dollar snowshoes. I put them here myself yesterday. Right here. Now, gone!" He waved his hand dramatically.

The policeman rubbed his chin and thought. "Snowshoes, eh? Well, that could be the work of teenagers, especially with the winter carnival coming up." Chief Greenway usually started out by blaming everything on teenagers.

Chris couldn't help protesting. "But sir, if it was kids, wouldn't they take more than one pair?"

The policeman only grunted in reply.

Then Chris remembered his manners. "Mr LePage, and Chief Greenway, I'd like to introduce my cousin Carol from the city. She's staying with us over the Christmas holidays."

The policeman nodded to Carol and went back to his checking.

Gratien LePage smiled, showing strong, even teeth under his black moustache. He held out a big hand. "I'm glad to meet you. How do you like our cold, eh, and the snow?"

"I just love it," Carol said, beaming. "And tomorrow the boys are taking me ice-fishing with them."

"Good. It's just the time for it. Gander Lake just south of town is good." He looked at Dumont. "You'll have things to do. I guess I won't need you here after all. I've decided not to open up until this afternoon. Run along with your friends."

But before Dumont had finished talking with his father, the phone rang. Mr LePage went into his little office, answered it, and then called, "It's for you, Chief."

The Chief spoke on the phone for a few moments, then came back with a grave expression on his face. "That was the mayor," he said. "There was another robbery last night. Bert Walker just called. Somebody smashed the back window of his store and took some canned stuff and cigarettes; no money, though." He looked hard at the boys. "Sounds like teenagers, all right. It's the fault of all this television crime."

Gratien LePage laughed a booming laugh. "A real crime wave on your hands, eh Chief? Biggest thing since the Samo Lake bank robbery."

"Well, we got those guys, didn't we?" the Chief said sharply. "Two shot resisting arrest, and one sent to the penitentiary." Then he grinned, realizing he was being kidded.

"But never found the money, eh?" LePage winked at the boys. "A million dollars, wasn't it?"

The Chief wasn't amused. "You know blamed well how much it was," he said. "A hundred thousand. No, we never did recover it."

"Say, you mean that really happened, Dad?" Dumont asked.

"Sure it happened," his father said, looking at him in surprise. "How would you know about it? You weren't even born. At least, let's see: ten years ago, well, you'd have been too young to take any notice anyway."

"Doodie Horton told us about it!" Dumont exclaimed. "We thought he was making it up. He said he held those guys single-handed till the police arrived."

Chief Greenway laughed loudly. "Well, he was certainly making that part up," he said. "Blamed old liar! He's got it the wrong way round, that's all."

"You mean he actually was involved, though?" Chris said eagerly.

"Sure, he was involved all right," the Chief said. "The three guys ran into the little trapping-cabin he used to have up north. The police were after them and they holed up there and shot it out. Your big hero Doodie Horton was lying flat on his face under his bunk the whole time the shooting was going on, otherwise he'd probably have been killed, too."

"Hey!" Chris said. "That's sure different from the way Doodie told it to us. You mean . . . ?"

But Chief Greenway suddenly seemed to realize that he was talking to two of his mortal enemies: teenagers, and cut off any further questions with a wave of the hand.

"I've got no time to waste on a ten-year-old robbery," he said. "What I want to know is who's responsible for these break-ins." He looked hard at the two boys. "And I'm going to find out."

An idea suddenly popped into Carol's mind. She gasped, fingers to mouth, and stared round at the store. "D'you suppose it could have been the muff . . ." she began.

But she never finished. Chris was on one side, Dumont

on the other. They each grasped an arm. "Come on," Chris said. "We've got to get over to Doodie's and find out about that lake."

Before the startled girl could protest, they had pushed her to the door and out onto the street.

5

An Old Friend Turns Nasty

On the street Carol shook herself free from the two boys. "Why didn't you let me tell about the muffled man?" she said, a little annoyed.

"In the first place Greenway wouldn't believe us," Chris said.

"And in the second," Dumont added, "we can't go round accusing people of crimes just because we don't like the look of them. We could probably be put in jail ourselves for that. That's what they call libel, or something. We'd better let the Chief solve his own crimes, even if he does think they're all caused by teenagers!"

"And dogs," Chris said, looking at Arthur and laughing.

"Come on, let's hurry," Dumont said. "We want to get to Doodie's place before lunch. He's such a friendly old guy he always wants us to eat with him."

"That would be fun," Carol began.

"No, that would be terrible," Dumont corrected. "Doodie's the world's worst cook. We stayed once and still haven't been able to decide what we had. I say it was wolverine fricasseed in skunk paste. Chris claims it was barbequed weasel."

"He sounds fascinating. I can hardly wait to meet him," Carol said, laughing.

"Oh, you'll like old Doodie," Chris said. "He's a great old guy. We go to see him almost every evening after school. You know, carry in wood for him, straighten the place up. He's pretty badly crippled with rheumatism."

"Not his tongue, though," Dumont said. "He sure has free and perfect use of that. He could talk the hind leg off a coyote."

"Are you going to tell him you've found out the truth about the bank robbers?" Carol said.

"Gosh, no!" Chris exclaimed. "If there's one thing Doodie doesn't take kindly to, it's being caught out in one of his tall stories. He gets as mad as a nest of hornets. He'd just throw us right out, and wouldn't talk to us for a week!"

They left the main street and followed a partly cleared path, which wound round an enormous, jagged chunk of rock as big as a house.

Behind the rock there was thick bush, consisting of evergreen and birch. A little way in, in a small clearing, sat Doodie's cabin. It was made of logs with white cement in between them. The overhanging roof, loaded with snow, reached down to within inches of the snowbanks in front. The path to the front door was not much more than a tunnel through the snow.

"Watch old Arthur," Chris said, pointing to the big dog, who had run ahead. "He always scratches at the door like crazy!"

But Arthur wasn't scratching at the door. Instead, he was sniffing round intently as though he'd found a scent that he remembered. The hair on the back of his neck began to rise and a half-snarl, half-growl, escaped from his throat.

Chris stopped in his tracks. "Now what in heck do you suppose is wrong with him?" he asked.

"Just a nutty dog, that's all," Dumont scoffed. "Can't help himself."

Chris said angrily, "He is not a nutty dog, and you know darned well he never fusses like this over nothing. Hey, d'you suppose anything could have happened to old Doodie? He'd be helpless if it did, you know!"

The two boys dashed towards the cabin and Chris pounded on the door.

There was no answer.

Chris pounded on the door again and shouted, "Doodie! Are you in there?"

Finally, there was an answer. "Of course I'm in here. What do you want?"

"It's Chris and Dumont. We've come to visit. You know, about that lake?" Chris felt a little foolish.

"He doesn't sound so friendly to me," Carol said.

"Oh that's just his way," Dumont said with a grin. He stepped over to the woodpile beside the path and loaded up with an armful of split pieces, knocking the snow off each piece before he piled it on his left arm. "This'll make him feel better."

Chris looked round with a half-puzzled, half-embarrassed grin. "Doodie," he called out. "Is it all right if we come in?"

There was no answer.

"Doodie?" Chris repeated.

"Come on let's go," Carol said, beginning to feel embarrassed, too.

"All right. Come in," the gruff voice said from inside the cabin. "The door ain't locked."

"I don't know whether we should," Carol whispered.

"For Pete's sake, why not?" Chris whispered back. "Doodie's our friend." He pushed the door open.

In the dim light from the two tiny windows at each end, Carol could see an enormous stone fireplace that filled half of the back wall and reached from floor to ceiling. On the wall on one side of the fireplace was a huge moosehead; on the other, the head of a five-point deer.

In front of the fire in an old-fashioned rocker with a robe over his knees sat an old, grey-bearded man. He had on a thick plaid shirt, with a sweater over the top of it.

The odour of the room was a mixture of wood smoke, old leather, and stale perspiration.

"I brought in some wood," Dumont announced cheerfully, heading for the woodbox by the old cook stove. He stopped in front of the box, which was already piled high with wood, and stared at it in amazement. "Oh, you've already got some," he said lamely.

"Got it myself," the old man said shortly. "What's wrong with that blasted mongrel of yours? You'd think he'd never been in this cabin afore."

They all looked at Arthur who was carefully sniffing the table legs, bearskin rug, couch, and even the washstand. Then he went back to sniff them all again. He hadn't even gone over to the old man in the chair for his usual pat and ear rub.

"Mr Horton," Chris said, ignoring Arthur's strange ways, "I'd like you to meet my cousin, Carol Fitzpatrick, from the city."

He'd expected the old man to brighten up and be a little

friendly. Instead, he merely grunted. "City, eh? What are you doing away up here?" He peered at her with his small dark eyes.

"Well," Carol stammered. "You see, my parents went to Bermuda. They were going to take me, but I said I'd like to come up and stay with Chris and his family." Then she added, "I just adore your fireplace."

"Takes a lot of wood," Doodie said, then turned to Chris. "Why don't you tell that fool dog of yours to lie down and mind his own business!"

"Oh, you know old Arthur," Chris said with an attempt to be pally. "He's the greatest sniffer in the district."

The old man didn't seem to hear. His eyes darted from one to the other.

He seems scared of something, Chris thought. He had an uncomfortable feeling of not being wanted, a feeling he had never had with Doodie before. He thought of the piece of paper in his pocket with the rough map on it, but now, for some reason, he hesitated to show it to Doodie. There was something wrong here: Arthur's strange behaviour, the filled woodbox, the old man's unfriendliness, and something else about the look of the cabin, though he couldn't quite think what it was.

The other two were looking at him, expecting him to begin. "Chris has something he wants to show you," Dumont began, but Chris cut him off.

"Uh, Dumont means I've got something to ask you: you know, about the bait, and the hidden lake."

"Hidden lake!" The old man jerked forwards. "I don't know nothing about no hidden lake."

"The one you said was full of fish that would bite like crazy in winter," Dumont prompted.

"Northeast of town?" Chris added.

"No!" The old man was positive. "Best place for ice-fishing is south of town where everybody else fishes. Now you kids stay out of those woods north of town! You'd get lost for sure."

The boys looked at him in amazement. The idea of their getting lost was so ridiculous they didn't even bother to argue about it.

"What about the bait you said you'd show us how to make?" Dumont asked.

The old man stared blankly. Then he fidgeted around in a way that reminded Chris of himself in school when he'd done something wrong and the teacher was staring at him. "Minnows," Doodie blurted out at last. "Use minnows. Best thing for ice-fishing."

Dumont started to protest indignantly but Doodie cut him off. "I'm not feeling well today," he said crankily. "Rheumatism's bad. You kids beat it, eh? Go on now. I don't feel like talking."

There was nothing else to do but leave. Outside the door Dumont exploded. "Well, I'll be a lake trout's uncle! What the heck gives with him?"

"So that's friendly, talkative old Doodie," Carol scoffed. "I'd sure hate to meet one of your grouchy friends!"

Chris was hopping mad. "What's wrong with him? He did so tell us about his lake north of town that was just full of fish!"

"Minnows yet," Dumont scoffed. "Some secret bait! Just what everybody else uses. Even those sportswriters that come up from the city know enough to use minnows."

"I wouldn't be sure," Carol said sweetly as they went back along the path, "but I've got an idea that old Mr

Whiskers back there has led you down the garden path. He probably never had any secret lake or secret bait at all. So how could he tell you about them?"

"No, that's not it." Chris stopped dead and kicked at the snow. "He was too positive about it before. We can always tell when Doodie's telling one of his tall stories and when he's telling the truth."

"That's right," Dumont said. "This wasn't any lie. For some reason he's suddenly decided not to tell us about it. There's something very queer about this."

"You know what?" Chris said.

"What?" Dumont asked.

"I bet we could find that lake. He told us before that it was four miles northeast of town, and between the big lakes. It must be marked on the Lands and Forests map, even if it doesn't have a name."

"That's right," Dumont said. "And the river runs out that way. That'd be a pretty easy route. We can follow it."

"You bet we can," Chris agreed. Then he turned to Carol and asked seriously, "Are you game for a hike into the woods?"

Carol drew herself up straight. "Anywhere you can go I can go, too!"

"Atta girl!" Dumont applauded.

"And wait until those softies back home in the city hear about this," she gloated.

Chris looked at her approvingly, then strode forwards, his jaw set determinedly. Imagine old Doodie giving us the runaround like that, he thought. Some friend. Well, we'll show him all right. We'll show him.

And so they turned for home, heading, without knowing it, towards the most terrifying adventure of their lives.

6

Preparations for the Bush

"Jeepers, look at all those lakes! " Carol exclaimed.

She and Chris were sitting at the kitchen table studying the large Lands and Forests map of the Canot area. It was three o'clock in the afternoon. Dumont was at home. Mrs Summerville had driven to the mine to pick up her husband.

"Yes," Chris said. "This country sure has 'em. When you look at it from an aeroplane you see as much water as land."

"What's this big one over here with all the squiggly bays and things?" Carol bent over to read the name. "Crushed Fly Lake! Now however did it get a kookie name like that?"

"Search me. Maybe something to do with the blackflies in spring. There are millions of them: they drive you crazy. At least we won't have them to worry about."

"What's all this green on the map?" Carol asked, running her finger over the spaces between the lakes.

"Bush, nothing but bush. See: there are no roads, not even a trail, just little rivers joining the lakes."

"Aren't there any mines up there even?"

"Not working ones. There may be some old abandoned ones. Dad says there was some mining up there about forty years ago, before there was even a town here. I guess some of the old tunnels may still be there."

Carol was studying the map again. "What's this dotted line with the little circles along it that comes right into town?" She ran her finger along it.

Chris looked at the explanation at the bottom of the map. " 'Power Transmission Line.' Oh yeah, that's the hydro line from the big dam away up at Kapawakabisha Canyon."

"Kap-a-walkaa . . . whata?"

"It's a big power development, away north of here. Where did you think we got our electricity from, to light the town and run the mines?"

"I never thought about it. And those power lines run right through the bush?"

"Yep. You can see where they branch off to go over to Samo Lake. That's the big town you came through on the way up."

"I never noticed it. I guess I was too interested in what Old Mufflers was doing. Do you see anything that looks like the lake you want?"

Chris's eyes were darting back and forth across the map. "You know, I think I do!" He pointed to a small blue speck between Crushed Fly Lake and Pine Lake. "Here, see this little feller? It looks almost like a bay on Crushed Fly Lake, but it isn't, and it hasn't got any name. Hey, we can follow the creek from town right up to Crushed Fly Lake and then go across the lake to this other one."

Carol leaned over and peered at the speck. "It doesn't look like much."

"Maybe not. But it's often the little lakes that have the most fish in them. Hardly anybody ever goes fishing in them, either."

"Is it far?"

Chris made a quick calculation. "No, only about four miles from here, even with the winding of the creek. That means eight miles altogether, there and back. D'you think you can walk that far?"

Carol looked at him scornfully. "I can hike as far as you can any day: ten miles, if you like."

In fact, Carol had never walked more than about four miles in her life, and then it had been on a well-worn ski or hiking-trail. She had no idea of what it was like to travel through the woods in winter.

She stood up and stretched. Then she glanced out of the kitchen window and screamed. "Help! It's Dangerous Dan himself!"

Chris stood up and looked out through the frost-covered window at a muffled figure shambling across the back yard. "That's Dumont, on snowshoes. He's very good on them. It looks as though he's got an extra pair slung over his back for you."

"Me? Snowshoes? I've never been on them in my life. Do I have to?"

"Nope, that is if you don't mind ploughing through snow up to your armpits. Out in the bush it's about three feet deep, even where it's level."

"Oh. I thought maybe I could go on skis. I'm pretty good on them."

A loud stamping on the back porch cut off further

discussion. Dumont took off his snowshoes and stamped through the back door into the kitchen. He was dressed in a long zippered coat with a fur-lined hood. On his back was a heavy knapsack, and on his feet a pair of cowhide moccasins, laced almost to his knees over heavy lumber-jack stockings whose black and white tops showed above the leather.

He raised a heavily mittened hand in a mock salute. "Private LePage, ready for the bush, sir. When do we go?" Then he looked round thoughtfully. "But first I must have something to eat. It is a long trek from my house to here, especially when I have to keep to the deep snow."

Chris opened the cupboard and brought out a can of cookies. "Okay, stock up." This was a pretty regular routine. Since Dumont's mother had died two years before, he and his father had had to share the house-keeping duties. As a result, he did most of his cake and cookie eating at the Summerville's: a situation that everyone, especially Mrs Summerville, accepted as right and just.

"Hey, Dumont, I think I've found Doodie's lake!" Chris said as Dumont began to chew. "Take a look at this thing that looks like a little bay."

Dumont leaned over the map. "Could be. Yep, sure could! Oh boy. Fish, here we come! When do we start?" he asked through a mouthful of coconut cookie.

"First thing in the morning, at sun-up." Chris looked at Carol, who gulped and nodded agreement.

"Say," Dumont said, dropping crumbs all over the map. "Where's that piece of paper with the muffled man's map on it? The way he was comparing them, the same place must be on this big map somewhere. We ought to be able to find it."

Chris produced the tattered piece of paper from his pocket and they went over it once more, comparing it with the big Lands and Forests map. But they got nowhere. The sketch was too roughly drawn. There just weren't enough details on it. It was impossible to guess what area it was supposed to represent.

"Well, even the muffled man seemed to be having trouble finding the place," Carol said. "He was looking at the two maps almost the whole time he was on the train."

"Oh, let's forget about the muffled man and his map!" Chris finally said wearily, putting it away again. "It's got nothing to do with us anyway. He's probably just some guy who's bought a piece of land up in the bush to build a fishing-cabin on or something. He's probably come up to look at it."

"In the middle of winter!" Dumont said. "Boy, he must really be eager to start building!" But he was tired of searching for the place, too, and leaned back in his chair.

"Dumont, how about you sleeping here with me to-night?" Chris said. "You know, so we'll all be together for an early start."

"Okay." Dumont nodded. It was so natural for him to do this that he didn't even remember to thank Chris for the invitation.

"Swell," Chris said. "Now let's make some plans."

The three of them sat down at the kitchen table with the map spread out in front of them and the cookie can handy. Although it was just three-thirty, the sun was low on the horizon and would soon be setting.

Chris stood up again and turned on the kitchen light. "The first thing to settle is whether we'll go on snowshoes or skis."

"Snowshoes are better in the bush," Dumont said.

"Not if you don't know how to walk on them," Carol countered.

"She's got a point there," Chris said. "We can all ski. How far do you think skis will sink in that snow, Dumont?"

Dumont shrugged and screwed up his long face. "Not more than three, four inches maybe, specially if we can follow that creek. We can take turns breaking trail and the others can follow in the track."

"Yes, and we can ski down any slopes we come to," Carol said.

"And if you fall down?" Dumont raised his eyebrows.

"You get up again."

"In three feet of soft snow? It's not so easy." Dumont shrugged, then noticed Carol's expression. It showed that she desperately wanted to go with them, but just as desperately didn't want to be a nuisance.

"On the whole I think skis will be best," he said. "We'll just have to be careful not to fall over."

Chris nodded, but he didn't feel right about it. He knew that as soon as you step into the bush you can be in danger, and going on skis was an extra risk.

"Okay," he said. "Now what should we take with us?"

Dumont fished in his pocket and produced a small pamphlet. "I have here the Department of Lands and Forests official Hunting Regulations," he said. "On the last page it gives some handy dandy hints about going into the bush. Number One." He cleared his throat. "Don't go into the bush without a good compass, and make sure you know how to use it. *Voilà!*" He dug into his pocket again and came up with a small pocket compass in a leather case. "One compass." He set it down on the table.

"Okay, Daniel Boone. What else does your handy dandy free booklet say?" Chris asked.

Dumont looked at it. "Be sure to take a good knife and a small axe."

"Got 'em," Chris said. Then he added, "What about a flashlight, or maybe two?"

"Whatever for?" Carol asked. "We won't be out at night."

"She's right," Dumont agreed. "It'll just make unnecessary weight."

Chris thought for a moment. Then he made a decision that later was to mean a great deal. "I don't know. We've got those ones that hang on our belts. They're no bother. Let's just take them."

Dumont shrugged agreement.

"Matches!" Carol exclaimed. "We must take matches."

The boys looked at her pityingly. "In waterproof cases," she added brightly.

"I guess maybe that's the first thing we learned after we learned to say 'goo,'" Dumont said, laughing at her, but not unkindly. "Chris will carry a tin box of matches."

One by one the items were counted off, including the lines and bait for fishing through the ice. Not a single item was forgotten. They even thought of taking a small silk tent that Dumont's father often used, but decided that that would be unnecessary.

"We've got far too much as it is," Dumont said. "We'll have to take a camel to carry it all."

"Hey!" Chris slapped his hand on the table. "Arthur! We can pile everything on my little three-foot toboggan and Arthur can pull it."

"And who's going to pull Arthur?" Dumont asked.

"Don't be funny. He's a good sleigh dog. And this will

give him practice for the junior dog-sled race at the winter carnival."

"Oh sure! And, boy, does he need practice!" Dumont threw up his hands.

"I think it's a wonderful idea," Carol said.

"Come to think of it, maybe you're right." Dumont winked at Chris. "Old Arthur can protect us from any timberwolves or wildcats we meet on the way."

Carol looked so startled that both boys burst out laughing. "Don't worry," Chris said. "There are plenty of wolves around, but they won't bother us, not in the daytime, anyway."

"Oh you two smart alecs!" Carol said, pouting. Then she brightened. "I'll take my movie camera and. . . ."

"Nope." Both boys shook their heads.

"My transistor radio?"

"Nope."

"But its very small. It fits inside my pocket."

Dumont shook his head, but Chris was thinking. "It might be a good idea at that. We could get the weather reports."

So they agreed to let Carol take the radio.

That evening Mr and Mrs Summerville went curling. The boys got together all the gear they wanted to take and piled it on the kitchen floor. But the pile got bigger and bigger and they had to begin to cut it down.

"In the first place, I don't see why we need four cans of pork and beans," Carol protested. "After all, we're only going to be in the bush for one meal."

Dumont was sitting on a low stool, knees wide apart, looking at the pile. "Do you know how much gas airline pilots take with them on every flight?" he asked.

"No. How much?" Carol said.

"Twice as much as they need. So, if they find that they can't get into the airport at their destination, they can turn round and fly all the way back to the airport they came from. It's a safety precaution."

"But we're not aeroplanes," Carol argued. "And we're not flying any thousand miles."

"Just the same," Chris put in, "we take the extra beans, and a package of wieners and some buns, and marshmallows, and a bag of cookies and a pot to boil water in, and some tea, and knives and forks. . . ."

"Are you going for a hike or a banquet?" Carol said. "How are we going to carry all that?"

"Arthur, remember?" Dumont said. "We'll load it all on the small toboggan with the other stuff. Don't worry, you'll be glad we've got plenty. Tramping through the bush sure gives you an appetite."

Chris stood up. "Right now we should hit the hay," he said. "We've got to set that old alarm for six o'clock."

By nine-thirty they were all in bed. Outside, the quarter-moon slid up over the tree-lined horizon and shone down on a frozen world.

It shone on a tiny, snow-banked cabin on the edge of Canot where an old bearded man squirmed in his second-best sleeping-bag and wondered how at seventy-six he'd managed to get into such a mess.

And farther north, it shone on a lone figure, muffled to the ears, shuffling heavily through the bush on snowshoes, carrying in his mittened hand a thirty-thirty rifle.

7

Skiing to Nowhere

Next morning the boys were up before the alarm went off. In their excitement they hadn't slept much, but neither of them felt tired.

Having gone to bed late the night before, Mr Summerville was still sleeping. But Mrs Summerville was up as early as anyone. While the boys loaded the toboggan, Carol helped her get breakfast.

"Aunt Mary, I don't know when I've been so excited!" she said eagerly.

Mrs Summerville couldn't help a frown of worry. "I do hope the lake isn't too far for you to walk," she said. "And please be careful not to fall through the fishing-hole in the ice."

"Gracious, don't worry about that," Carol said, laughing. "I just hope I won't make too many mistakes and make the boys think I'm a complete goon."

Mrs Summerville smiled at her niece and turned to the stove. "Don't worry. Tim will show you what to do."

Carol looked up, puzzled, but before she could ask who Tim was, Chris and Dumont burst in at the door.

"We're all set!" Chris yelled. "Let's go."

"Nobody's going anywhere until you've eaten this bacon and eggs," Mrs Summerville said firmly. "Now just sit down and have a good breakfast."

They sat down, but they didn't have a good breakfast. They were far too excited. And when they got up most of the bacon and eggs was still on their plates.

Before Mrs Summerville could protest again, Dumont and Chris had left the table and were out at the back struggling to get Arthur into his harness.

Carol came out onto the porch and took a deep breath. "Ummm," she said. "Just smell that cold, crisp air. It makes you feel good to be alive."

Dumont leapt up onto the porch and took a quick look at the thermometer. "Hey, it's gone up," he said. "Just about zero now. Just right for ice-fishing."

Chris was inspecting the toboggan on which their heap of gear was now tied. "That axe," he said. "It looks to me as if it might fall off. I think I'll carry it." He took it off the toboggan and pushed it, handle first, through his belt, so that it stuck out like a sword. "Let's go," he said.

They worked their ski boots into the cross-country harness on the skis, and started across the back yard. The sun was up a little way now, and each of them cast a long shadow on the pure white snow.

At the end of the yard there was a trail through the bush leading to the creek. In the summer, it was a path that the boys used to get to the water, but now it only showed as a space between the trees.

The skis sank about three inches into the snow. Chris, who was in the lead, jammed his ski pole down into it as far as it would go, and then pulled it out again. He put his hand on the pole where the top of the snow had been, and measured it against his body.

"Almost to the waist," he said. "And I didn't have that pole right down to the ground either."

"I saw a picture of a rhinoceros stuck in a mudhole in Africa once," Carol said. "I guess that's how you'd feel if you fell over in that snow."

Dumont was bringing up the rear. "This rhinoceros behind me isn't having much trouble," he said, looking back at Arthur, whom he was leading on a leather strap, and who was pulling the small toboggan as if it weren't there.

Arthur wagged his bushy tail. He was happy to be going with the boys, happy to be pulling the toboggan: in fact, just happy.

When they reached the creek, the going was somewhat easier, though in places there were dead branches or trunks that they had to go round or over.

After a while, Carol called to Chris to stop and, when he did so, she caught up with him. Dumont pulled alongside, too.

"What's wrong?" Chris asked. "Tired already?"

"No." Carol was serious. "I just thought of something. Before breakfast when I was talking about fishing, Aunt Mary said that Tim would show me how. What did she mean? Who's Tim?"

"Holy catfish!" Chris exclaimed. "Tim Beaton. He has some huts on Gander Lake south of town. I bet that's where she thinks we've gone. I remember now, we never did tell her we were going to fish on this other lake."

"Does it matter?" Carol asked. "I mean, would she mind us going to this other one?"

Chris didn't answer at once. He knew that his mother probably would object to their going to a lake where they would be on their own. But they had come too far now. And anyway, it was a fine day: nothing was going to happen to them. "What about your dad?" he said to Dumont.

Dumont thought for a second. "I told him we were going ice-fishing, that's all. I guess he thinks we're going to Gander Lake, too. That's where everyone goes."

"Well, they'll all be surprised when we come home loaded with fish, that's all," Chris said. "Come on, let's go!" But somehow he wished he had remembered to tell his parents where they were going. He really had meant to.

He started off in the lead again, and the going was so good that within the next hour they covered about two more miles along the creek. The sun rode low over the treetops; there was no wind.

"The thing to watch for along here is worm holes," Chris shouted back to Carol. "Holes in the ice under the snow made by beavers or the current. If a person ever got a wet foot he'd be in really bad trouble."

And then, Dumont, who had fallen behind, called for a halt. "I've got to fix my ski harness," he said. Arthur sat down to look at him, and Dumont dropped the leather leash on the snow and shook off his mitts.

And then fate, as though thinking that the group was having things too easy, turned against them. A big snowshoe rabbit, who happened to be loping along through the woods, suddenly changed course and leaped down onto the creek bed.

Arthur let out one delighted yelp and gave chase. Dumont called, "Hey, stop! Arthur!" But by the time the dog passed Carol he was in full stride, barking crazily.

Chris saw him coming, shouted and tried to get in his way, but only succeeded in falling on his face in the snow. When he lifted his head, rabbit, Arthur, and toboggan had disappeared around a bend in the creek.

"Arthur! Come back here!" Chris shouted from where he lay on the snow, wiping the snow off his face with his mitt. And then he raved like a madman at the dog. "You blasted, boneheaded, slab-sided, good-for-nothing piece of crow bait, come back here!"

The sight of Chris floundering in the snow and helplessly roaring at the dog was too much for Carol. She laughed so hard that she, too, stumbled over into the snow.

Only Dumont was mobile. Calling frantically to the dog, he ski'd past his two fallen friends and disappeared round the bend of the creek after Arthur.

By taking his skis off, placing them side by side on top of the snow and climbing onto them, Chris was able to get back on his feet. Then, in answer to Carol's giggling pleas, he ski'd back and helped her to her feet. When she saw his grim, red face, she stopped laughing.

"You won't think it's so funny if we lose all our gear," Chris said. "Come on."

He set off with long strides, pushing himself on with his ski poles as much as the deep snow would allow. But when he got round the turn of the creek there was no sign of Arthur. He could hear his excited yapping somewhere off to the right, as he continued in pursuit of the rabbit.

Dumont was working his way with difficulty up the side of the creek bank. "Come on," he yelled. "There's a kind of trail here, probably an old pulp trail. They went down there."

"Wait for me," Carol called frantically from behind. "Wait for me."

But Chris knew that he mustn't wait, not long anyway. Once Arthur got on the trail of a rabbit he didn't stop until he had caught it or was exhausted. Their only hope was that the toboggan might get caught against a tree before everything was flung off it.

"We're going up here," he shouted back to Carol. "Come on as fast as you can!"

Chris worked his way up the bank, side-stepping on his skis and using the poles to support himself. Once up, he started off along Dumont's track, going as fast as he could.

The narrow clearing through the woods led straight out from the creek for a hundred yards or so, then turned and became more vague as it continued through small birch and poplar.

Dumont stopped at the turn, knocked the two-foot-high snow cap off a stump and sat down on it, his skis on either side. He was puffing very hard when Chris reached him.

"How do you like that for the bonehead play of the season?" Dumont shook his head dejectedly. "I let go of him!"

"It wasn't your fault," Chris said. "It was just bad luck that the rabbit came when you were fixing your ski." He shook his head. "We'd better wait for Carol here. I'm too pooped to go on for a while, anyway."

When Carol came up with them, she was almost played out, too. She had pushed her parka back off her head and unzippered her jacket.

But she hadn't lost her good humour. "Where's the runaway?" she asked.

"He went thataway." Dumont pointed to where the toboggan track showed lightly on the snow.

"As soon as we get a little rest we're going after him." Chris looked at his wrist watch. "Gosh, it's only ten o'clock. From the way my stomach feels I thought it must be twelve."

"Me, too. I'm positively starved," Carol agreed.

Dumont had thrown his head back and was looking up through the trees. "What do you know about that?" he said. "It's clouded over."

"So it has," Carol said. "Where did those clouds come from so fast?"

"Oh they'll do that all right," Chris said. He didn't like the look of it. A slight wind was stirring the tops of the trees. "Come on," he said, "let's find that crazy dog before the weather gets bad. I'll break trail."

He started off, but now the going was much more difficult. Every few yards they had to detour round trees and white hummocks of snow. Besides, unlike the surface of the creek, the ground here was very uneven, making it impossible for them to travel in a straight line.

"What are all these big bumps all over the place?" Carol asked when they finally stopped for breath. They seemed to have travelled a long way in the last little while, twisting and turning.

"Rocks," Chris told her. "You should see this country in the summer: it's practically all rocks."

Dumont lifted his head and shouted as loudly as he could. "Here, Arthur! Here, Arthur! Here, Arthur!"

But there was absolutely no sound in reply. The only

sign of life was a bird, about the size of a robin, flitting silently from one evergreen to another. "Look at that big grey bird!" Carol exclaimed. "What is it?"

"Whiskey Jack," Dumont told her. "Or Canada Jay some people call it. They always hang around you when you're in the bush, looking for a handout. As soon as we start eating lunch there'll be one practically sitting on our shoulders."

"Please, please!" Carol pleaded. "Don't talk about food. Was every bit of it on that toboggan?" She flicked off a large snowflake that had landed on her nose. "Hey, it's beginning to snow!"

Chris looked up at the patch of sky he could see through the trees. The clouds were lower, packed in a grey mass. It was going to be one of those grey winter days, he thought, when visibility was poor and the snow heavy.

"I think we'd better get back to the creek," he said quietly. "No sense in following the dog any farther. He can find us a heck of a lot easier than we can find him." He lifted his right foot and swung his ski at right angles to the way they had been heading.

Before he could swing the other ski alongside it, Dumont spoke up. "Why are you turning that way?" he said.

"To get back to the creek, of course."

"It's not over there. It's over this way!" Dumont pointed in the opposite direction.

"You're crazy!" Chris said. "Don't you remember? We made a turn back there at the big birch."

"But before that we made another turn. Isn't that right, Carol?" Dumont twisted round and looked at her.

Carol shook her head and looked from one to the other. "You know something pretty crazy: I'm not sure!" She tried to remember the way they had come, but it all seemed muddled. "Wouldn't it be better to follow our tracks back?" she said.

"No, we don't have to do that," Chris said. "We've been twisting and turning all over the place. We'll be worn out if we go back over all that ground. The creek's not far from here, and once we hit it we're okay. Let's go this way first. If we don't get to it soon, we'll come back and try the other way. It must be in one direction or the other!"

Dumont agreed, and so they started out in a straight line to the right. But almost at once the look of the ground changed. They found themselves going uphill, through bush that was becoming thicker and thicker all the time.

Finally they had to stop to rest again. Carol's skis had begun to slide backwards along the track and she would have fallen over if she hadn't managed to wrap her arms around a small tree.

"I may be just a city-type girl," she said panting, "but don't creeks usually flow in low places? How can we find it by going uphill?"

"I think you've got a point there," Chris agreed. "We'll go back, but we'll rest a bit first."

It was snowing heavily now, and as the flakes hit the bare branches of the trees they made a faint whispering sound. The temperature had risen, too, so that all three of them felt like taking off their outer jackets.

"This is the most beautiful sight I've ever seen!" Carol exclaimed. "All the stumps seem to be wearing tall snow-white fur hats."

"Yeah, pretty," Dumont replied. "But the most beautiful thing to me right now will be that creek. Come on, let's go back."

But it was even more difficult going back downhill than it had been coming up. If they followed in the track they had already made, the skis went too fast for safety in the heavy bush. So they had to go off at an angle, and once again the ground changed. Nothing looked the same, and each new slope meant a change of direction.

After about fifteen minutes of this Chris called a halt. Dumont could tell that he was really worried, in spite of the fact that he was smiling for Carol's benefit.

"You know something?" he said cheerfully. "I think we missed our turn. Say, Daniel Boone, what did we bring that compass for, if not to see which direction is which."

"Compass?" Dumont's face fell about a foot. He quickly felt his pockets. "I haven't got it. I thought one of you. . . ." His voice trailed off as he looked at the other two imploringly.

They shook their heads.

Dumont tried his best to be casual. "Well, well, imagine that: no compass!" But it didn't come off.

Carol's voice sounded almost pleased. "Now don't you two woodsmen tell me that we is lost."

There was no amusement in Chris's voice. "Yeah," he said. "We is lost!"

8

The Clue in the Drawing

"When lost, stop, sit down. Try to figure out where you are. Use your head and not your legs."

Dumont was reading from his handy dandy book of hints for hunters. The three of them were sitting on a fallen tree from which the boys had scraped the snow. Inside each of them a small serpent of fear had begun to uncoil, but each of them was determined not to let it grow.

"Well, that's one instruction we can follow," Chris said. "What's next?"

Dumont read on. "When going into new country, always carry a map."

"Oh, heck!" Chris burst out. "Why in the name of galloping snowflakes didn't I bring that map of Dad's that we were looking at yesterday!"

"No map, no compass," Dumont said, shrugging. "So far we're wrong on two out of three. Let's see what's next."

He ran his finger down the page. "If lost in unknown territory, find a stream and follow it." He scratched his head. "Yep, that's good advice, all right. But if we could find the stream we wouldn't be lost."

"What's next?" Carol asked. The snow, which was falling even more heavily now, had turned her blue parka almost white.

Dumont read on. "Don't follow old wood roads; they generally wander around aimlessly and lead nowhere." He looked at Chris.

Chris shrugged. "Now he tells me."

"Oh here's one we can really follow," Dumont said cheerfully. "Listen to this, 'Don't yell, don't run, don't worry, and above all, don't quit!'" He slammed the booklet shut and stuffed it back into his pocket. "So much for the don'ts. Now we could use some do's."

Chris looked at Dumont and Carol and thought about their situation. It was serious. They were really lost: at least two miles from home in unknown woods without food, and without a clue as to which direction was which. He looked at his watch. Twelve-thirty. There were at least three more hours of daylight and then about one more of dusk before it became pitch dark.

And where was Arthur? He seemed to have disappeared completely. If the toboggan had caught on a tree or something he'd be stuck.

As though reading his thoughts, Carol said, "You don't suppose somebody could have caught Arthur, do you?"

Dumont snorted. "Fat chance! If there's anybody out here, I wish they'd catch us."

"If we could all look after ourselves as well as Arthur, we'd be all right," Chris said. "Now I suggest that we start using our heads, the way the man suggested in the book."

"I second the motion," Dumont agreed. He squinted up at the snow-laden trees and the falling flakes, which had cut visibility almost to zero. "I think maybe if we go downhill in a straight line we'll come to a lake. This country is full of them."

"What do we want with a lake?" Carol asked.

"Well, it'll be flat and at least we'll be able to see past the end of our noses on a lake," Chris said.

The idea of doing something made them all feel better. "It's very important that we travel in a straight line," Chris said. "Otherwise we'll just go round in circles. I suggest we spread out. Dumont, you go first, then Carol about twenty-five feet behind you, and me another twenty-five feet behind her. We should be able to see that far through these trees. And if you wander to either side, Dumont, I'll be able to tell and holler at you."

It was a good plan and it worked.

Slowly they edged their way down the side of the slope. Each time Dumont detoured around a rock or fallen tree, Chris directed him back to the straight line. Then, when they had gone about half a mile, Dumont shouted, "Here it is!"

The other two hurried down onto the edge of what looked like a flat plain covered with snow. It could only be a lake.

They were standing in a little bay, and on one side of it they could dimly see a rock cliff. The top was covered with snow and trees but the grey granite showed on the side. It stretched out into the lake as a long point covered with towering pine trees. Straight out past it they looked into a wall of falling snow flakes. For all they could tell, the lake might be one mile wide or ten.

"Well, we've found the lake. What now?" Carol said, puffing from the march through the bush.

Chris had no answer. As he peered vainly out into the white curtain of snow, he tried to remember his father's map. He remembered Crushed Fly Lake, all right, but it had so many bays and inlets, facing in so many different directions, that it was impossible to remember which was which.

"What do you say, Dumont?" he asked. "Is there any point in trying to cross the lake?"

"Not while it's snowing, I'd say," Dumont replied. "We can't see where we're going and nobody could see us."

Carol didn't say anything. She had moved back into the shelter of some trees and had taken a small pad and pencil from her pocket. Now she began to draw on it.

"This is a fine time to get artistic," Dumont said, as he and Chris followed her. "What are you doing?"

"Just sketching what I see." Carol went on with her work. "There doesn't seem to be much else to do."

"Hey, I didn't know you could draw," Chris said, peering at the book. The side of the cliff was taking shape in rough outline, along with the bare white birch trees and snow-covered evergreens. "Gosh," he said. "That's swell! Have you got any more?"

Carol flicked back a couple of pages, keeping the book out of the falling snow as much as possible.

Dumont peered over to have a look, too. "Hey, that's a picture of the muffled man!" he exclaimed. "That's exactly what he looked like: muffler, hat, and everything!"

"Why didn't you show us this before?" Chris said.

"There hasn't exactly been much time," Carol explained. "I only did them last night."

"What else have you got?"

Carol flicked over another page to a sketch of the

inside of Doodie's cabin, showing the fireplace, moosehead, deerhead, and all. The boys' eyes were wide with admiration.

"You mean you do these from memory?" Dumont said in astonishment. "How do you remember so much of what you see?"

"Just practice, I guess," Carol said. "I've been drawing like this ever since I was little, and we had one art teacher at school who used to make us remember the things we saw. He would put a lot of things on a table, like an orange and an apple, some paint brushes and a lot of other different things, and then he would make us turn around and draw what we had seen, without looking at it again. When we had put in everything we could remember, he'd let us look at the table again to see what we'd forgotten. It's a way artists have of training themselves to notice things. I'm going on to art college when I leave school."

Chris was looking at the drawing of Doodie's cabin with a frown of concentration. "Well, there's one thing you didn't remember, though," he said. "Doodie's knapsack, that he keeps hanging on those deer horns over the fireplace."

"For Pete's sake!" Dumont exclaimed. "You don't expect her to remember a little thing like that, do you? She was only in the cabin a few minutes!"

"No, that's not what I meant," Chris said, still frowning. "I knew there was something different about Doodie's cabin when we were in there last night, and now I know what it was. The reason Carol didn't remember that knapsack was that it wasn't there!"

"Say, that's right!" Dumont said, after a moment's thought. "And you know something else that was missing, that's always there? Now I remember noticing it, and then not thinking anything about it."

"What?" Chris said.

"His best sleeping-bag, the red one that's always on the bed," Dumont said. "His old green one was there. I remember noticing that the bed was a different colour!"

"Well, what does that mean?" Carol said, looking up in astonishment at the excitement in their voices. "Maybe he sent his red sleeping-bag to be cleaned, and threw his old knapsack away!"

"No, not Doodie!" Chris said emphatically. "He never throws anything away, especially not his old hunting-equipment."

Dumont laughed. "And he doesn't get things dry-cleaned, either. That red sleeping-bag's been on the bed for almost as long as he has!"

"Well, what's so important about it, then?" Carol said, wrinkling her nose slightly at the thought of the sleeping-bag.

"Somebody had taken them! That's what it means!" Chris said. "And now that I remember how old Arthur acted around that cabin, I've got a darn good idea who it was!"

"Right!" Dumont said excitedly. "The only person who's made Arthur growl and bristle that way lately was the one who stepped off the train right in front of you the other night!"

"The muffled man!" Carol said. "But whatever has he got to do with Doodie? Are they friends or something?"

Chris was thinking. "You know, it struck me Doodie was scared of something when we went to see him. That could have been why he acted so queerly."

"You mean you think the muffled man was hiding right there in the cabin somewhere all the time we were there?" Carol said. "Where could he hide?"

"No, that's impossible," Chris said. "There isn't room for anyone to hide in there, and if he'd actually been anywhere around, old Arthur would have sniffed him out. But he sure as shooting had been there, I bet anything."

"But whatever would a character like that have to do with Doodie?" Dumont said in a puzzled voice. "You don't suppose the old coot's in cahoots with him?"

"Not old Doodie!" Chris protested. "He may be a liar but he's no crook! I bet Doodie didn't lend that stuff to him."

"It seems a funny kind of robbery," Carol said. "A sleeping-bag and an old knapsack."

"Yeah," Dumont said thoughtfully. "Except if that's what you happen to need." He paused. "As well as a pair of snowshoes, a thirty-thirty rifle, and some sticks of dynamite!"

"And some canned food and other stuff!" Chris added. "That's right! He could have been responsible for that break-in at your dad's store, and at Bert Walker's, too."

"Well!" Carol exploded. "When I suggested that, you pretty well dragged me out of the store by the hair!"

But the boys ignored her complaint. Dumont had had another idea.

"You know the other thing Doodie really seemed to get het up about?" he said. "Us coming up here and looking for his lake. D'you suppose that had anything to do with the muffled man? All that stuff that was stolen would be just what someone would need if they were coming out into the bush. Maybe he made Doodie tell him about that lake, and Doodie wanted to keep us away from it. . . . Aw, but that doesn't make any kind of sense!" he said. "Why would anybody go to all that trouble, just to go fishing?"

Chris shook his head too. There had to be more to it than that, but maybe only Doodie knew what. He'd certainly wanted to keep them away from the lake, though, that was sure, and it certainly seemed to have something to do with the muffled man.

Carol laughed nervously. "Well, if that's so, maybe it's just as well we did get lost and didn't find the lake, if that character is there and up to something illegal! Maybe we'd just better stay lost, and hope we don't discover the lake by mistake!" She looked down at the lake in front of them anxiously. "Could this be it?"

"Naw," Dumont said. "This is much too big to be the one Doodie talked about. Anyway, there's no sign of anybody round here." He looked round him grimly and added, "Worse luck!"

Chris suddenly shivered in a blast of wind and shook himself. Dumont was right. It might even have been better to have run into the muffled man, if he could have told them how to get back, than to stay out here lost in the bush with a bad snowstorm coming on. Dumont knew the bush better than Carol and knew that it was at least as dangerous an enemy to them at the moment as any muffled man could be.

What they had to do right now was keep warm. It was no use trying to go on travelling while it was snowing so heavily. They would have no idea where they were going, and their tracks would be covered up immediately.

Dumont seemed to read his thoughts. "Know what I think?" he said. "We should stay right here, and build a fire: at least until the snow stops, which it should do in an hour or so."

He didn't look at the others as he said this. Chris knew that there was no real reason why the snow should stop within an hour, or even that day. But he refused to think about what that would mean.

"Good idea," he said cheerfully. "Let's move back up a bit."

Up to this point, looking after themselves in the bush had been an exciting game. Now it could be a matter of life and death.

9

A Camp in the Snow

In front of them the bank sloped up into the trees. About twenty feet up was a flat piece of ground on which stood four large jack-pine trees. Among them were a number of white birch, some dead, some living. A thick clump of spruce stood over to one side.

"If those pines are normal," Chris said, "the bottom branches should be dead. The twigs should be dry as match sticks."

"Come on," he shouted to Carol. "Let's get up to that little clearing. We'll make a fire under those pines. Take your skis off here."

Without a word Carol removed her skis, and immediately sank to above her knees in the snow.

"Come on," Dumont urged. "It isn't easy, but it isn't far. We'll go first; you follow in our tracks." Each step was an effort. They lifted their feet as high as they could and plunged them forwards. By the time they reached the clearing, they were puffing heavily. Carol was still struggling up the slope.

Underneath the largest pine, Chris and Dumont got down on their knees. With their mittened hands they scooped out the snow until the dried pine needles showed. It was hard work. Every time they dug a handful of the soft snow out, some more slid back into the hole. But finally they managed to clear a circle about two feet across.

Carol had reached the clearing now and Chris saw that she was very tired. "Sit down in the snow for a while and catch your breath," he said. "There's nothing you can do yet."

Now Dumont ploughed his way over to the nearest birch and began to peel off some of the top layer of paper-thin bark that was sticking out from the trunk in several places. He stuffed this in his pocket.

Chris, meanwhile, had moved over to a pine tree. He reached up, and caught hold of the end of one of its dry branches. It was about ten feet long and about two inches thick where it grew out of the trunk. He jerked downwards and the branch bent. Then with a snap it came off, dropping all its snow on him.

He carried the long branch with its thin dry twigs over to the fireplace and stood it up in the snow. Then, taking off his mitts, he carefully broke off the tiny end twigs, keeping them in his hands.

Dumont came back to the hole in the snow and placed the little handful of birchbark on the ground gently. Then, one by one, Chris piled his tiny twigs on top of it in the shape of a miniature tepee.

Now for the real test. The whole success or failure in lighting a fire lay in the first minute. If they could get those little twigs to catch, then build it with larger twigs, they would have a fire.

Chris unzippered his jacket, reached into his inside

pocket, and brought out the small square tobacco tin in which he carried the matches.

He pried at the lid with his finger nails. It was stuck. He pried harder. Then, with a snap, the lid flew off and all the matches spilled into the deep snow.

"Blast it all!" he exclaimed, lurching forwards to catch them and failing. Instead, he only succeeded in throwing snow all over the small, precious pile of bark and twigs! For a moment, as he crouched in the deep snow and looked at the mess in front of him, he felt like crying. Dumont, who had been standing behind him, said quietly, "I'll get some more birchbark." Carol said nothing. As Dumont plodded away, Chris groped in the snow with freezing fingers and found two of the matches. The ends were wet. How could he light a wet match?

Holding the ends of the two matches between his teeth, he gingerly picked his mitts up out of the snow and wriggled his freezing fingers into them. Then he banged his hands against his sides to get them warm again.

Carol stood up and came over towards him. "I don't want to tell you your business," she said softly. "But if I were you I wouldn't light a fire under that big Christmas tree anyway."

"Why not?"

She pointed up to the branch ten feet above his fire-place. Along the upper side of it lay a pad of snow that must have weighed over a hundred pounds. "I read a story once about a man who lit a fire under a pine tree. The heat melted the snow a bit and it all came down on his fire."

Chris could have kicked himself. She was right, but it

didn't help to have her tell him. "If you're so smart," he said, "maybe you know how to light wet matches!"

"No, but I can dry them," she said. She took the matches from his hand and, pushing back her parka, began to rub the heads through her long hair. "I read about this in a book, too."

Chris stared in amazement: a city girl teaching them the tricks of the bush! But, immediately, he was on his knees again, digging a place for the fire away from the tree. Dumont came back with his birchbark, and they began again. Again Chris broke off the tiny twigs and stood them up over the birchbark. Carol handed him a match.

He took it and bent over very carefully, so as not to disturb bark, twigs, or snow. Then he struck the match along the metal band of his watch. Nothing happened. He struck it again. The match burst into flame. Very gently, he lowered it onto their precious little pile of bark and twigs, holding his other hand over it to keep off the falling flakes.

As he touched the flame to a shred of birchbark, it began to burn with a dark smoke. The little twig on top caught fire immediately and curled up and the fire spread to others.

Now to keep it going.

With great care the three of them broke more twigs from the dead branch, which was standing in the snow beside them, and, one by one, laid them in criss-cross patterns on the fire. They were careful not to put on any that were too big.

The pine twigs were so dry and so filled with resin that they burned like oil, and the fire grew. "It's going!" Chris said, slowly letting out the breath he'd been holding. "You feed more of these little pieces of wood on, Carol, while we get some bigger stuff. And be careful not to knock any snow on top of it!"

A half-hour later the three of them sat in front of the roaring fire and toasted themselves. It was still snowing heavily.

The big fire had melted back the snow from around it. Nearby was a large pile of broken dry branches that Chris and Dumont had collected. Most of the rest of the snow in the camp area had been packed down by their tramping back and forth over it.

The thoughts of all three of them were different.

As he half lay, half sat, with his feet propped up on a log, Dumont was not happy. This thing was mostly his fault. He had dropped the leash and let Arthur go. He had left the compass behind. He was a dope.

Carol's feelings were a mixture of bewilderment and fear. Were they really lost? Was this how it happened? One moment they were walking along in the sunlight, perfectly safe, with lots of food, and knowing exactly where they were; the next, they were squatting like Indians beside a fire, lost in the deep bush, with no food and no shelter. And out here somewhere in the bush with them, perhaps, was the weird and frightening muffled man, whose every action was a mystery.

Chris was thinking more practical thoughts. They were lost all right. And with his folks and Dumont's father thinking they had gone to Gander Lake, nobody would think of looking for them up here. They'd have to get out of this mess themselves. The snow was falling faster. It was absolutely impossible for them to travel. They'd have to stay out in the bush all night.

"You know something?" he said. "The Cree Indians used to live in this country all winter long. We read about it in our social studies."

Carol brightened. "Yes, and they didn't have metal axes or knives, either, not before the white men came. What did they live in anyway?"

"Wigwams," Dumont said unhappily. "Made of poles covered with skins or birchbark."

Chris stood up and looked round. Although it was just after three in the afternoon, it was already dusk.

"We haven't time to make a proper wigwam, even if we could," he said. "But I bet we can make a shelter." He pointed to a mound of snow not far to the right. Beside it was a small, natural cave made by the swirling snow.

"There's a big fallen tree there with a hollow under it. If we dig more snow out and pile it up, and then lay all our skis and ski poles over it, and cover it with pine and spruce boughs . . ."

Carol was on her feet, her face flushed with excitement. "We'd have a sort of half-wigwam, half-igloo effect. Do you think we'd be warm enough inside it?"

"If the weather stays like this we will," Dumont said, feeling a little better. "As long as it keeps snowing it isn't likely to get much colder."

"And we can hollow out the snow in front of the door and put a fire there," Chris added. "Now that we've got one going, it won't be hard to start another from it."

"Hand me a ski, Carol," Dumont said. "The mighty woodsman is about to swing into action."

Chris pointed to the clump of black spruce twenty-five feet away. Their branches drooped right down to the ground. "These are the best for roof material," he shouted, ploughing towards them. "I'll cut off a bunch with the axe."

Dumont moved over to the mound and began to scoop out the snow from under the tree trunk with his ski. Carol followed his example.

The space under the fallen trunk proved to be even deeper than they thought. The large tamarack had grown too heavy for its roots in the thin, rocky layer of soil, and had toppled over. The trunk was about two feet thick and showed no sign of decay. The other trees that it had fallen on held it about four feet off the ground.

As Carol scooped the snow out, she said happily, "I've always wanted to sleep in a snow house, but when does a city gal ever get a chance!"

"Push the snow back this way," Dumont advised, "so that it'll make a wall." The hole got deeper and deeper and soon dead pine needles and bits of bark were showing on the ground.

Chris staggered over with a bundle of spruce boughs. "That looks great," he said, and started back along the path he had made for another armload. Inside the hole, Dumont and Carol were now lifting snow as high as their shoulders to pile it on top of the wall. The bottom was practically cleared.

"Now for the skis," Dumont said. "You hand them to me and I'll lay them across the top from the inside. Be careful not to knock our wall down."

Carol got the six skis and the six poles. Dumont laid the skis carefully across from the tree trunk to the bank, leaving a space of about a foot and a half between one ski and the next. It made a shelter nine feet long and about five feet wide. Then he placed the ski poles lengthwise, across the skis.

Chris arrived with another load of boughs, and walked carefully round to the side of the hole where Carol and Dumont were working. The deep path they had made in the snow looked almost like a tunnel.

Very carefully, stretching their arms as far as they could, the two boys laid the spruce boughs on top of the skis and ski poles. As soon as they had used the ones that Chris had brought, which were enough to cover about half the roof, they went back to the spruce clump for more branches. And then, when they had completely covered the roof, they brought several more loads to cover the floor inside the shelter.

By the time they were finished it was quite dark. The dancing flames of their fire, which they had kept stoked, cast long shadows through the bush.

Now they cleared a space in front of the open end of the shelter for a new fire, just far enough from the entrance to avoid the risk of setting fire to the spruce boughs.

When that was finished, the three of them stood for a few moments in the flickering light of the fire. For the first time, they began to feel completely forlorn, alone and lost. Besides, they were desperately hungry. They'd had nothing to eat since their early breakfast, and what they would have given now for the eggs and bacon and toast that they'd been too excited to eat then!

Dumont tried to make a joke. "Anyway we don't have to hang up our clothes tonight." But it fell flat.

"We're going to need an awful pile of wood to keep that fire going all night," Chris said finally, snapping out of his blue mood. "Come on, let's get it."

There was plenty of dead wood around, but it was hard work dragging it through the deep snow into camp and cutting it up. When they finally decided that they had gathered enough, they were so weary they could scarcely stand. And, although none of them complained, they were hungrier than they had ever been in their lives.

Chris built the new fire carefully, from birchbark to small twigs, to bigger sticks, to good-sized pieces and, finally, logs. Altogether the wood made a tepee-shaped pile about three feet high.

The boys flipped a chip to see who would take first turn sleeping by the door and keeping the fire going. Chris lost.

Dumont and Carol got down on their hands and knees and crawled into the shelter. Before following them, Chris took a flaming stick from their first fire. Then he crawled backwards into the shelter, holding it, and shoved it deep into the bottom of his new pile of wood. The birchbark caught immediately and soon the fire was going well.

"This is the life, eh?" Chris said, after a few minutes, as he snuggled down on top of the spruce branches. But he got no answer. The other two were already asleep.

He lay on his side and looked at the fire. People out in the cold weren't supposed to go to sleep for fear of freezing to death, he remembered. Surely it wasn't cold enough for that. But he could feel his feet beginning to tingle. What if the fire went out when he fell asleep? They might all freeze!

Then he heard it: a sound in the woods, a far-off rustling and scraping. Something was out there and it was coming closer. But what could it be? Animals, he knew, never approached a campfire at night. But perhaps a

man . . . ! The thought of the muffled man, somewhere out in these woods suddenly came back to him.

He remembered the axe and could have kicked himself for leaving it sticking in a piece of wood at the other side of the fire. His heart was thumping so hard that he could feel it in his neck.

The sound was coming closer and closer. From where he lay he suddenly saw a large black shape beyond the fire. It was breathing heavily. And then the shape became familiar.

"Arthur!" Chris said with a gasp of relief.

With a whimper the big dog moved towards the mouth of the snow cave. Chris could see that he was dragging the small toboggan along upside down by one trace and, in typical Arthur style, looked as if he were going to drag it straight through the fire.

As quickly as he could, and without waking the others, Chris crawled out of the shelter and grabbed him. Arthur sat down on his bushy tail and, as Chris leaned over, tried to lick his master's face.

Chris hugged the big shaggy head. "Good old pooch," he said. "Good, crazy old pooch. Boy, am I glad to see you!"

Then he turned the small toboggan over. The knapsack was still lashed to it. Arthur had dug into it and eaten the wieners and buns. But one lone can of beans was still there!

Chris untied the harness and eased Arthur into the snow cave, and, as if he knew how to be of most use, the big dog immediately spread himself over the feet of Dumont and Carol.

Chris put some more logs on the fire. Then he crawled in and shoved his own feet under the dog. Already they felt warmer. And in the morning they would eat, even if it was only a can of beans.

He went to sleep.

10

The Search

Slowly and very carefully Mrs Summerville hung up the phone. But she couldn't keep her hand from shaking slightly and her face was drawn into worried lines. With a great effort she kept her voice calm.

"Alec," she called, getting up from the phone stool and going into the living-room.

Alec Summerville looked at her over the top of the paper he was reading. "Yes?"

"That was Tim Beaton I was talking to on the phone. He just got back from the lake. He says the boys weren't out there today."

Alec Summerville frowned and put the paper aside. "Then they must have decided not to go ice-fishing after all. They probably went skating."

"They left here at dawn this morning, on their skis, and with all their equipment for ice-fishing."

"Then they must have changed their minds before they got there. It wouldn't be the first time. Maybe they're at Dumont's place."

Although his voice was casual, Mr Summerville got up immediately and went to the phone. In a minute he was back. "All that Gratien LePage knows is that they were going ice-fishing. He says they must have been out at Gander Lake and that Tim Beaton probably didn't see them."

"No," his wife said firmly. "He was positive there was nobody at the lake when he left. He said it was snowing so heavily that everybody packed up and left." She moved to the window and drew back the curtain. "Alec, it's snowing even harder. Where can they be?"

"My guess is that they're in town somewhere and that they'll show up in a few minutes wondering what all the fuss is about." He looked at his wife. "Please sit down, dear. It's no use upsetting yourself."

"But they may be out in the woods somewhere, lost or injured! They should have been home hours ago. It's been snowing since ten o'clock this morning. Why aren't they home?"

Her husband shrugged helplessly. "I think I'll do some phoning around. They may be at the Harrises' or the Grahams'." He walked towards the phone.

It was several phone calls later when Alec Summerville finally decided that they must be at their old friend Doodie Horton's, forgetting the time as they listened to his yarns. But Doodie didn't have a phone, so Mr Summerville had to walk out to his cabin, leaving his wife to go on with the phoning.

His journey was wasted. The old prospector could only tell him, rather abruptly, that he hadn't seen the youngsters since the previous day and that all he knew was that they planned to go ice-fishing.

It was seven o'clock by the time he had come back and

made a few more phone calls. His last phone conversation had been with Chief Greenway. He hung up the receiver and walked wearily into the living-room.

"The Chief says they can't do anything until morning."

"Morning!" Mrs Summerville turned from the window. "But that means they might be out all night!"

"I'm afraid it does. But Greenway's right. There's nothing anybody can do until daylight. He's organizing a search party for tomorrow. They'll cover the whole area south of town. The Department of Lands and Forests here has radio'd out for its plane and they say they can get a helicopter if necessary."

"But what about tonight!" Mrs Summerville's face was white. "What can we do tonight?"

Her husband put his arm round her shoulders. "All we can do is wait," he said quietly. "They may still come in. Luckily it's not very cold. Chris and Dumont know enough about the bush to look after themselves." He tried to smile, but it didn't work.

There was no sleep in the Summerville household that night. There was not much in Doodie Horton's cabin, either. Late into the night, the old prospector hunched over the fire, staring into the glowing embers, worrying.

The worry had started soon after Mr Summerville had left. If Chris and Dumont and that girl cousin from the city really were missing, and if they hadn't been to Gander Lake that day, it could mean that the little fools had set out to try to find his lake, after all.

And if they had headed that way: north, instead of south, he shuddered to think of the reason why they might be missing. He knew only too well whom they might have run into in that direction!

11

The Abandoned Tower

"Oh give me a home where the buffalo roam
And the deer and the antelope play . . ."

The man's voice woke Chris with a start. Who was he? And where was that music coming from?

He looked out of the snow cave. It was still snowing a little. There was Dumont piling wood on the already blazing fire. And there was Carol sitting on a log, combing her hair. Beside her, her tiny blue and white transistor radio was blaring away.

"Well, I'll be . . . !" Chris squirmed from underneath Arthur, who was lying almost on top of him. "Where did you get that thing?"

"It was in my jacket pocket all the time," Carol shouted above the music. "I forgot all about it in the excitement."

The music stopped.

"Good morning to you one and all," a cheery voice said. "This is the Happy Harry Show, and old Harry's here with weather reports, time signals, good music, and tips on how to get that sleep out of your eyes."

Then the voice changed. "But first here is an important

message. The three young people, two boys and a girl, who went into the bush in the neighbourhood of Gander Lake yesterday morning have not yet returned. Anyone who has seen them or who has any idea of their whereabouts, please contact the Chief of Police in Canot immediately. Chief Greenway and the Department of Lands and Forests are organizing an extensive search of the whole area south of Canot where the children are believed to be. They were accompanied by a large black-and-white dog pulling a toboggan. This station will give bulletins on the progress of the search every half-hour."

"South of town!" Chris breathed without looking at the others. "Boy, how stupid can a guy be?"

"The weather forecast for today," the voice went on, "is for more snow, with increasing winds from the north, colder with some drifting. And now for our morning march!"

A brass band burst into the rousing strains of a military march.

"Boy, the wonders of modern science," Dumont said. "Now we know we're officially lost, we know what the weather's like, and we know that people are looking for us where we're not."

Carol moved the radio on the log to make room for her mitts. The sound faded.

"Hey!" Chris exclaimed. "Turn that thing again, a little this way!"

Carol did. Again the sound was clearer.

"What does that prove?" she asked.

"It proves that Samo Lake's in that direction." Chris pointed. "The radio's always louder when it's at a right angle to the direction of the sound wave!"

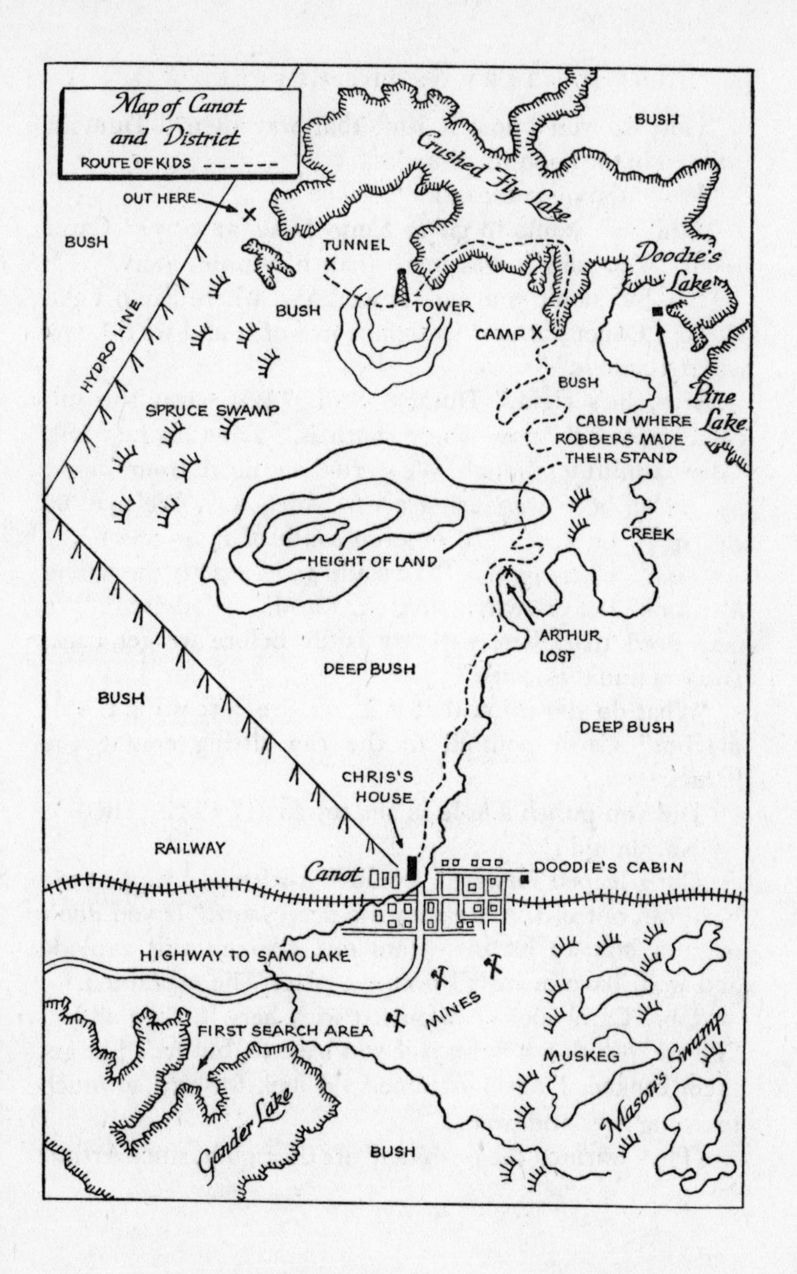
Map of Canot and District
ROUTE OF KIDS
OUT HERE
BUSH
Crushed Fly Lake
BUSH
TUNNEL
TOWER
Doodie's Lake
BUSH
CAMP
HYDRO LINE
BUSH
Pine Lake
SPRUCE SWAMP
CABIN WHERE ROBBERS MADE THEIR STAND
CREEK
HEIGHT OF LAND
ARTHUR LOST
DEEP BUSH
BUSH
DEEP BUSH
CHRIS'S HOUSE
RAILWAY
Canot
DOODIE'S CABIN
HIGHWAY TO SAMO LAKE
MINES
FIRST SEARCH AREA
MUSKEG
Mason's Swamp
Gander Lake
BUSH

"How do you know it isn't that way then?" Dumont pointed in the opposite direction.

"Well, it's one or the other."

"And who wants to go to Samo Lake, anyway?" Carol asked. "You said it was more than fifty miles away."

"No, but don't you see? If we know where Samo Lake is, well, Canot's almost straight north of it and we'll know where Canot is."

"Hey, he's right," Dumont said. "And when the sun comes up we'll know where south is." Then his face fell. "Wait a minute, though. We started out north from Canot, but we've been wandering every which way. We may be east of it, or west of it, or even south of it by now!"

"Yeah," Chris agreed. "We could go in exactly the wrong direction. Better switch that off, Carol," he advised. "We may need that battery pretty badly before we get back. Did you find the beans?"

"What do you think that is in the fire, a roasting rabbit maybe?" Carol pointed to the can sitting among the flames.

"Did you punch a hole in the top first?" Chris yelled.

"No. Should I?"

Chris leaped forwards, grabbed a stick and flipped the bean can out of the fire into the deep snow. "If you don't make a hole to let the steam out, the can will explode and we'll have beans all over the place," he explained.

"Oh." Carol looked disgusted with herself, then added, "Please, punch a hole in it if you have to, but let's just get them cooked. I never dreamed I'd look forward so much to eating pork and beans!"

They warmed the beans and ate them, but, since Arthur

had managed to lose everything else off the toboggan, they couldn't make any tea.

"My mother always told me not to eat snow," Carol said, making a face as she chewed at a handful. "I don't think she'll ever have to tell me again."

"Now," Chris said when they had finished. "The next question is, where do we go from here?"

"I suggest we go out onto the lake and see what we can see from there," Dumont said. "Maybe we can find the creek and follow it back to town."

"We certainly can't keep to the bush," Chris said. "It's too tough travelling: we never know where we're going."

So they went down to the lake to look round them. Straight out from the bay they were in, perhaps half a mile away, was an island. They decided to ski out around the point for a look at the rest of the shore.

The skiing was good on the lake, but it was cold. Now that they were away from the sheltering trees the wind cut their faces. The wind was getting stronger, too, and already the new snow was slithering across the flat surface. A blizzard, Chris thought: that's all we'd need!

When they had passed the point they stopped, sheltered their faces from the wind with their mittened hands, and peered round the shore of the lake. The heavy forest came down to the shore everywhere without a break. There was no sign of a creek, no sign of a house or person or track. They were absolutely alone.

Suddenly Dumont lifted his hand and shouted. "Look! Away over there, back from the shore! It looks like a tower!"

The others looked where he was pointing. "It is," Chris agreed. "It could be a forest ranger tower."

"The map!" Carol yelled.

"What map?"

"That map the muffled man had, you bucket head. There was something like a tower marked on that!"

"Never mind about that now," Chris said. "We could see for miles from the top of that thing. Maybe we could even see Canot! Come on, let's go!"

The tower was about a mile away across the ice and maybe another quarter of a mile up the bank. It was an hour later before they stood at the bottom of it, completely winded.

It had obviously been deserted for years. There wasn't a building near it and, peering up, they could see that the shack at the top had blown off, leaving only the wooden platform.

"Shivering salamanders, are we going up that thing?" Carol said. "It doesn't look very safe to me."

Chris tapped the metal ladder with his ski pole. It gave out a ringing sound. "Solid enough," he said.

"Well, let's go up and see what we can see," Dumont urged.

Carol bent her head back and looked up. "Not this girl," she said. "That thing must be a mile high!"

"It's only about a hundred feet," Chris corrected.

"What's the difference? You'd be just as dead when you hit the bottom."

Chris was patient. "There's really nothing to it, Carol. The trick is not to look down until we get to the top. Then we look out over the countryside. We'll need you up there to make a sketch of what we see," he added.

Carol looked at the two boys. "You make it sound pretty simple."

"I'll go first, and then you, and then Chris," Dumont said. "Then if you fall. . . ."

"Uh uh uh," Chris interrupted. "Let's stop talking and start climbing."

Dumont kicked off his skis, stepped onto the ladder and ran up about ten rungs. Carol followed.

But much to Chris's bewilderment, soon after he had started up he began to feel funny. His knees seemed strangely weak. He swallowed hard, looked up and climbed after the others.

"Hey, this isn't bad!" Carol yelled. "I can see over the tops of the trees!"

Above her, Dumont had hooked one arm round the ladder and, shading his eyes with his free hand, was looking out over the landscape. "That's sure a big lake," he said. "It's just full of islands."

From below Carol, Chris shouted desperately, "Don't stop! Don't stop! Keep climbing!"

"Okay, okay," Dumont called down. He moved on up the ladder, his ski boots ringing on the iron rungs. Carol was right behind him.

On the ground, Arthur, tied to the bottom rung, pulled on his leash and barked crazily.

At the top of the ladder there was a hole, leading through to the square wooden platform. Once there had been a trap door there, leading into the little cabin.

Dumont wriggled through the opening and crouched on the platform. Carol climbed through and sat down quickly. With nothing above or on either side of her, she suddenly felt very shaky.

Chris squeezed through the hole with great care. His face was pale and he seemed to have trouble breathing.

He didn't kneel or sit on the platform, but stretched out full length, gasping for breath.

At this height the wind was three times as strong as it was down below. It made a whining noise as it blew through the metal girders. It was beginning to snow again and on the lake they could see the snow drifting steadily.

Looking down at the solid bush, Carol realized why it had been impossible for them to find their way through it. And there was certainly no sign of a town.

On one side, about a mile away, a high ridge cut across their view and the blowing snow made it impossible to see anything beyond it.

"Maybe the town is over there," Dumont shouted above the wind. "But then again, maybe it isn't. I don't see any sign of that blasted creek!"

On the ground, a hundred feet below, Arthur stood with his front paws on the ladder, looking up, whining and barking.

But Carol wasn't paying attention to the dog or the boys. "Look," she said, pointing down towards the lake. "That line of trees and rocks along there, that must be the shore."

"Sure," Dumont said. "That's where we've just come from."

"Chris," Carol said breathlessly, "let me see that drawing. Do you have it on you: the one that the muffled man dropped?"

Grumbling, Chris rolled onto his side and fumbled about in his pockets for the paper. "Here," he gasped. "I don't know why you're still bothering about that. We've got worse things than the muffled man to worry about." He rolled over, face down on the boards again.

But Carol refused to be put off. She began to look at the rough map, then at the landscape below.

"Yes sir," she said. "This could be it! See that line there? Well, look over there to our right. Doesn't that look like this line on the drawing?"

But Dumont showed no interest whatsoever. "Right now, I'm not interested in anything I can't eat," he said. "Those poor little lonesome beans are rattling around in my stomach crying for company."

"Oh, you and your stomach!" Carol scoffed. "I tell you this looks just like the area marked on the muffled man's map."

"You could find a thousand places that look like that," Dumont said. "That drawing's so rough that it could be practically anywhere."

"But this tower really could be the ladder thing marked on the map," Carol persisted. "And that would mean that this place that the muffled man has marked X could be somewhere over there." She pointed to their left along the lake.

Chris remained strangely silent, lying on his stomach and pressing himself against the boards.

Suddenly Dumont, who had been looking in the direction in which Carol had been pointing, banged him on the shoulder. "Say, look down there!" he yelled.

Chris didn't raise his head. "I . . . I can't look down," he said quietly. "It makes me feel dizzy."

"What is it, Dumont?" Carol said, trying to follow his glance.

Dumont was peering through the falling snow. "I think it's smoke!" he said. "See, coming from that tamarack grove about half a mile away."

"Yes, I see it," Carol said. "Not much smoke, but some."

"And where there's smoke there's people," Dumont exulted. "There must be a cabin down there: probably a trapper, or ice-fisherman, or an Indian, maybe."

But Carol had gone suddenly quiet after her first excitement. She gazed in the direction of the smoke, and then looked back at the rough diagram in her hand thoughtfully. "Or else it could be our friend," she said softly and ominously, tapping the map with her hand.

"The muffled man?" Dumont said, looking at her seriously for the first time.

"This certainly looks to me like what was shown on his map," Carol said. "And if it is, that place where the smoke is coming from could easily be the spot marked X."

Dumont took the map from her and looked at it a moment, then back at the thin line of smoke, which kept disappearing in the falling snow. "I suppose so," he said slowly. "But so what? Perhaps he does have a cabin up here after all, and that was what the map was supposed to show. Just because he looked kind of queer and didn't like old Arthur, we've been imagining that he was some kind of master crook!"

"Well, what about the broken arm that wasn't broken?" Carol said quietly. "Or the way he ran at the sight of the Mounties? Or what happened at your friend, Doodie Horton's?"

"Okay, so there's something peculiar about him," Dumont said, shivering in an icy blast of wind that made the tower sway. "But at least he's human, and if that is him he must have food and some kind of shelter. He's not going to eat us! We can either try and get help, and risk meeting the muffled man, or we can stay out here until we starve or freeze to death!"

Carol was silent for a moment, then she said, "I guess so. What do you say, Chris?"

But Chris, who had been unusually silent all this time, and who was still stretched out flat on the platform, merely shook his head. "I don't care," he said.

"Come on, let's get down out of here then," Dumont said briskly. "I don't like the way this old tower is swaying. You go first, Chris, then you, Carol, then me."

But Chris didn't move.

Dumont looked at him. "Come on, let's get going before this thing blows over."

Chris raised his head and looked at Dumont. And in that look his friend saw what he and Carol had both failed to see up to now: stark, helpless terror.

"I can't, Dumont," Chris gasped. "I just can't. I'm scared!"

12

On the Track of the Smoke

A quick laugh burst from Dumont's lips. "Scared?" he said unbelievingly. "Who, you? What of, the muffled man? You're kidding!"

"Wait a minute, Dumont." Carol was looking at Chris with real concern. "What's the matter?" she asked quietly.

"I don't know. I feel terrible. I have ever since we began to climb the ladder."

"You are kind of pale," Dumont said, looking at him closely. "You're not sick, are you?"

"Kind of." Chris shook his head as if to clear it. "I can't look down. In fact, I can't even think about looking down."

"Are you sure you're not kidding?" Dumont said doubtfully. "This is no time for jokes, you know."

"No, wait a minute," Carol said. "Some people do have a fear of heights. I've read about it. They just can't stand being up in any high place."

"You mean you think Chris is like that? Why didn't it ever happen before, then?"

"Well, maybe he's never been up anywhere high like this before. Have you, Chris?"

He shook his head.

"Well, I guess that could be, too," Dumont said. "The highest place in town is only about three storeys, and I don't suppose he's ever been up on the roof. But what do we do now? We can't leave him up here. And we can't carry him down."

"I'll get down, don't you worry." Chris forced himself to sit up. But at that moment the tower swayed again in a gust of wind and he cringed back down on the floor.

Dumont's eyes were big with concern now. He crawled over and patted Chris on the shoulder, then looked at Carol. "This book you read, did it tell you how to cure this thing?"

"Of course not. There isn't any cure. The only thing is not to climb anything high."

"Now she tells us. So people just have to go around until one day they find they've got this thing and then they're stuck, up the top of a mountain or something!"

The wind was getting stronger now, and colder. It seemed to cut right through their jackets. The tower swayed dangerously.

"The trouble with us," Dumont muttered disgustedly, "is that we just go ahead and do things without thinking. We see a tower, *voilà,* we climb it! But how are we going to get down? We never give it a thought!"

"If we had a rope . . . ," Carol began and then stopped They didn't have a rope.

"One thing is sure," Dumont said, keeping his back to the wind. "We've got to get down out of here fast. If ever I saw a blizzard coming, this is it. If we wait much longer we won't even be able to find that tamarack grove where we saw the smoke."

Chris gritted his teeth. "Just keep talking to me," he said. "Tell me some jokes, make me mad, but keep talking. Don't give me time to think about anything. And get moving!" he said fiercely.

"Good boy! I'll go first," Dumont said. "You follow me, and Carol can bring up the rear. Just keep climbing. Don't stop, and don't look down."

"Okay, okay, okay," Chris said impatiently. "For Pete's sake start climbing!"

Dumont was through the hole like a chipmunk. He went down about five steps and then stopped.

Grasping the ladder with numb hands, Chris followed. His knees felt so weak that he wondered for a moment if his legs would hold him.

"Keep coming," Dumont shouted, and went down two more rungs.

Chris's breath was coming in painful gasps. He could hardly resist the desire to throw his arms round the ladder, clutch it to his chest and never let go of it. "Mustn't do it," he mumbled to himself. "Got to keep climbing, got to. . . ."

From above him Carol shouted encouragement. "Keep going, Chris, keep going! You can do it!"

The wind was even stronger. The sway of the tower was now quite noticeable.

Down below Arthur jerked at his strap and barked his loudest.

"Arthur's pulling for you," Dumont shouted up at Chris. "He. . . ." Dumont never finished that sentence. A heavy ski boot landed on his shoulder and almost knocked his hands off the metal rungs of the ladder.

He managed to hang on, and looked up. Chris, white-faced and staring, was clutching the ladder for dear life.

"Okay, okay!" Dumont called. "Keep coming. No harm done. We'll soon be at the tops of the trees."

And somehow, painfully, with Dumont talking all the time and Chris staring straight ahead, they made it.

As soon as his feet touched the ground, Chris released a long, tired sigh. "Boy, that's the last time anybody gets me on anything higher than a footstool!" he said. "Of all the kookie things for a guy to do." He made his way over to a fallen tree and sat down on it heavily.

"Don't worry about it," Dumont said. "Good thing you're down, though. I was running out of jokes."

And that was the last that was said about the incident.

After a moment's rest, they fastened on their skis. Even among the trees the wind was strong enough now to make them burrow their noses into their parkas.

Dumont pointed with his ski pole. "The smoke we saw was straight in that direction."

"How far do you think it is?" Chris asked.

"I'd say about half a mile."

"D'you think we should go by way of the lake?" Chris said. "Might be easier than going through the bush."

"I don't think so. I'm not sure that I could find the place from the lake. I've got a kind of bearing on it from here."

So, very carefully, they figured out the exact direction of the smoke and decided to spread out again so that they could travel in a straight line.

Chris took first turn at breaking trail. At first the going was fairly easy. They were travelling slightly downhill through white birch and poplar, with, here and there, a towering pine or tamarack.

But when they had gone about a quarter of a mile they ran into the thickest of all northern bush: a black-spruce swamp. The trees were not tall, only thirty to fifty feet, and their trunks were mostly less than ten inches thick, but they were growing so closely together that the lower branches formed an almost solid wall.

Chris stopped and the others caught up and leaned wearily on their ski poles. Carol was puffing hard. She took off her heavy mitt and pushed back a wisp of loose hair. But the wind was so cold that she immediately put the mitt back on again.

Chris looked at her with concern. "How about it, Carol?" he asked.

She grinned weakly. "Oh I'm doing fine, just fine. Why are we stopping?"

Chris pointed forwards with his ski pole. "We can't possibly go through that."

"You said it!" Dumont agreed. "And we can't stand around much, either. We're pretty warm right now from skiing, but we'll soon cool off in this wind."

"Right." Chris tried to sound matter of fact, but the situation, he knew, was desperate. Carol was beginning to look exhausted and they were all weak with hunger. They simply had to get help soon. "The way I look at it," he said, "this may be just a small swamp of black spruce. No one would camp or build a cabin in there, so the smoke you saw must have come from somewhere on the other side of it. The ground's a bit higher over to the right. I suggest we go up that way as far as we have to and work our way round the side of the swamp."

"It's the only thing to do," Dumont agreed. He grinned at Carol. "Don't worry. In a little while we'll all be in a nice warm cabin in front of a big fireplace eating roast venison."

"Don't talk about it, boy, lead me to it!" Carol exclaimed, straightening up with an effort.

Deliberately, they had all avoided mentioning one possibility. Instead of a nice warm cabin and roast venison, what they might find waiting for them at the place where they had seen the smoke was the ever-mysterious muffled man. But the thought of him was constantly at the back of their minds now, like a threatening cloud.

Chris desperately hoped that they were doing the right thing. But, really, they had no choice. They had to get to food and shelter and help. Otherwise, well, it was at least fifteen degrees colder than it had been the night before. He knew that spending another night in the bush would be an entirely different story.

"I'll break trail this time," Dumont volunteered. He swung right, swerved to avoid a large, snow-covered rock, and started through the birch and evergreens up the slope.

Then he disappeared.

Chris was getting hold of Arthur's strap, ready to follow. Carol had already started along Dumont's trail.

"Dumont!" she gasped. "He disappeared!"

Chris looked ahead in amazement to where Dumont had been, then dropped the leash and ski'd past Carol up the slope.

Then he stopped abruptly. He was on the edge of a twelve-foot cliff, which had been completely hidden by an enormous pine tree that grew up past it from down below. Dumont's tracks led right over it.

At the base of the cliff, beside the trunk of the pine tree, there was a hole in the snow where Dumont and his skis had completely disappeared.

13

Doodie's Story

Noon, December 22nd of that year, was the worst time the new mining-town of Canot had ever known.

Through the streets, weary, grim-faced men, dressed in their warmest clothing and carrying snowshoes or skis, hurried from the southern outskirts towards the town hall in the centre of town. They met other not-quite-so-weary men, also carrying skis or snowshoes, hurrying away from the town hall towards the bush.

Most of these men had been searching the bush since early that morning. Many had had no breakfast. Each man, as he came out the town hall door, looked up at the grey skies, felt the rising wind on his face, and drew his lips into a thinner, grimmer line.

Inside the town hall, which was the headquarters of the search operation, some of the men, who had come back in and made their reports and who were waiting for further orders, were sitting on chairs or leaning against the walls, still in their parkas and snowboots. Four of them wore the uniform of the Royal Canadian Mounted Police. One of them, and perhaps the most worried of all, was Doodie Horton, who had hobbled down to the hall early in the morning and who had been hanging around there ever since, as the reports came in.

Everyone was watching the Chief Forest Ranger from Samo Lake, who was standing with Mr and Mrs Summerville and Gratien LePage in front of a large aerial map of the district.

Heavy dark lines had been drawn across the map, dividing it into sections.

"Now we've covered all this area in here in the neighbourhood of Gander Lake," the Ranger said, running his finger over it. "And there's no sign of them. And we've covered this area in here and still no sign of them." He looked hard at the men who had come in last and they nodded their heads in confirmation.

"Okay. Now, we know they're somewhere south of town. That's where they headed and in the time they've been out they couldn't have got very far." He drew in a deep breath and shifted his finger to the right side of the map. "So that leaves this piece in the southeast." It was a large area that showed dark and unbroken.

One of the Mounties shook his head. "Do you really think they could have got into Mason's Swamp, George?"

The Ranger looked at him. "They could have, Jim. Like you, I'm hoping they didn't. Looking for anybody in there is going to be like looking for a snowflake in a blizzard. But they've got to be somewhere."

Another voice spoke up. "No use kidding ourselves. If they got lost in the snowstorm they could wander into the swamp as easy as not. One thing, sleeping out last night, if they did, they'd have plenty of shelter in there from the spruce."

The others shook their heads. This was little consolation.

"Okay," the Chief Ranger went on. "Unless somebody's got a better idea, I'm suggesting we concentrate on Mason's Swamp from now on. It'll be all foot work. We can't get a ski scoot or a snowmobile in there, no matter what we do."

One of the Mounties spoke up. "The helicopter should be here in another hour, but it won't be much use over that spruce swamp, either."

"Well, if we've got to hit the swamp, let's hit her!" A big, red-faced man in a fur-lined jacket stood up. It was Harry Longknife, a purebred Cree Indian who knew the bush better than any man. "Don't want any storekeepers or barbers going in there alone, though," he said. "Or we'll be looking for more than three people."

It was at this moment that Doodie Horton finally won the struggle with himself that had been going on all morning. He pushed himself up off his chair at the side of the hall and began to hobble towards the front.

"Hold on a minute!" he called out. "I got something to say before you all go off gittin' yourselves mired in that swamp."

All heads turned towards the old prospector and one or two of the searchers laughed.

"Come on, Doodie!" one of them called out. "We've got no time to listen to your stories now!"

There was a general laugh at this, but Doodie burst out, "This ain't no story! I think you've all been searchin' in the wrong direction, an' you jest better listen till I tell what I got to tell!"

There was a buzz of conversation now, as Doodie reached the front of the hall and began talking more quietly with the Chief Ranger and the youngsters' parents.

"Mr Summerville," Doodie said, looking up at him with his watery blue eyes, "I mean it: it might be you're looking in the wrong place for them kids."

"What do you mean, man?" Gratien LePage demanded.

Doodie moistened his lips. "I think your kids went north of town."

Mrs Summerville gasped. "North! Why do you say that?"

"Because it could be they were looking for a lake I was tellin' them about, a little place near Crushed Fly."

"You sent the kids north, into the bush?" Gratien LePage said angrily. "By golly . . . !"

"Just a minute, Gratien," Alec Summerville said. "What do you mean, Doodie?"

"Course I didn't send them north! I told them not to go. I even pleaded with them! But they may have gone jest the same. You know what kids are." He stopped.

Mrs Summerville went white. "Alec! They said something about Doodie's lake! I remember now. But I didn't pay any attention!"

Gratien LePage stood over the old man. "You old fool," he stormed. "Why didn't you tell us this sooner? For half a day men have been searching south of town!"

The old man looked up at him. "I didn't know for sure they'd gone north! They might have gone south to Gander Lake and got lost for all I knew. But now you've searched all that part, except the swamp, I guess they didn't. Besides. . . ." He stopped again.

"Besides what?" Mr Summerville said.

But Doodie shook his head. "This is jest for Chief Greenway," he said. "Where is he?"

Chief Greenway at that moment was on the phone, but

one of the searchers was sent to find him, and in a few moments he was back in the hall.

As soon as he came up to the platform, Doodie asked to speak with him privately, and the two of them went to one side, talking in low tones, while the youngsters' parents looked on anxiously.

In a moment, the Chief called the Chief Ranger and the four Mounties over, and the seven men went into a serious huddle in one corner.

All that Mr and Mrs Summerville and Gratien LePage could hear above the now excited buzz of conversation from the hall, were a few isolated words.

"I tell you, he threatened to kill me!" Doodie shouted excitedly. "Said he had friends who would do it for him if he couldn't."

"Muffled!" the Chief exclaimed. "You mean you didn't actually see his face?"

". . . bandages . . . ," from Doodie. "No doubt about who it was . . . killer. . . ."

After a few more minutes of excited conversation, the group in the corner broke up and Chief Greenway came to the front of the platform, holding up his hands for silence.

"All right!" he said. "We're going to switch the direction of the search: up north, around Crushed Fly Lake. But before we start, I want all those of you who have got weapons at home to go home and get them and then report back here. I'll provide arms for anyone without a gun.

"This time we may be searching for a killer as well!"

14

Into the Earth

Chris and Carol stood on the edge of the small rock cliff looking down in horror at the hole where Dumont had disappeared.

"Be careful!" Chris warned. "You can't see the edge of this cliff. The snow hangs about a foot out over it. Dumont went through the overhang!" He pointed to the marks where Dumont had slid sideways, taking a great deal of snow with him.

"But where is he?" Carol's voice was desperate. "There's just a big hole down there!"

"Dumont!" Chris called. "Are you all right?"

There was a stirring at the edge of the hole down below. Then a snowman poked its head out. It was Dumont.

He was pushing the snow away from his body with his hands as if he were swimming. "I think so," he puffed. "Nothing broken . . . except one ski. But there's a sort of cave down here under the snow, and a sort of tunnel!"

"A tunnel? What kind of tunnel?" Chris shouted.

"I don't know, but it seems to go away back. It's awful dark in there."

"What do you think it could be?" Carol asked, shivering against the biting wind.

"I don't know: unless it's an old mine tunnel. Sometimes they're dug into the side of a cliff like this. I don't mean the shaft: that goes straight down, but maybe an exploratory tunnel. Most mines have three or four entrances."

A weary voice came from below. "What's going on up there? You just going to stand talking? Come down and give a guy a hand."

"Okay. Sorry," Chris yelled. "We'll be right down."

He turned to Carol. "The best way to get down there is to take off our skis, throw them down, and then jump into the soft snow to the right of Dumont."

At any other time, jumping off a ten-foot cliff into a four-foot snow drift would have seemed like fun. But now, cold and hungry and miserable as they were, it seemed just another ordeal. They unhitched Arthur and threw down the skis and toboggan, then jumped to the other side, with Arthur following.

They sank almost up to their armpits and had to lie down and half crawl, half swim, towards the hole where Dumont had again disappeared.

Chris crawled into the mouth of the tunnel, hauling his skis, the toboggan, and Arthur. Carol floundered after him, her skis in her arms.

Dumont was on his hands and knees on the snow-covered rock just where the tunnel began, gazing sadly at his broken ski. "Now I've either got too many legs or not enough skis," he said. "I've loused things up again."

"Anyway," Carol said, "down here we're out of that awful wind!"

Chris was examining Dumont's ski. "Like it or not, this

is where we're going to stay. We can't travel through this snow without skis." For the first time, he felt hopeless. They would have to have food soon. He looked at his two companions, sitting huddled on the rock floor. "If we move back a little farther into this tunnel," he suggested, "we'll be completely out of the wind."

Dumont was undoing the flashlight from his belt. "Thank goodness we brought these," he said, aiming a shaft of light into the tunnel. The walls were of solid granite, and curved upwards to a ceiling about eight feet from the floor. Patches of frost were clinging along the tunnel wall.

Carol shuddered. "What a grisly looking place!" She got wearily to her feet. "But, as you say, it may be warmer farther along."

Cautiously they ventured into the tunnel which slanted down at an angle of about thirty degrees. The noise of their ski boots on the rock floor echoed off the walls. Arthur ran on ahead, eager as always to explore this new place.

When they had gone about thirty feet into the tunnel, Carol stopped. "At the risk of appearing slightly chicken," she said, "I've got to admit that I don't like this place. Don't mines cave in sometimes? I've read about them doing it."

"Not these hard rock mines as much as coal mines," Chris explained. "Dad's told me that there isn't much danger of that, especially in granite like this. There are places where the rock isn't as solid, though, where the ceiling and the walls have to be held up with timbers."

Dumont was looking down the tunnel and sniffing. "I may be crazy as a wet hen," he said, "but I think I smell something like bacon."

"Bacon!" The other two sniffed the air like hungry wolves.

"There is something there," Chris said. "Anyway, it smells like food of some kind."

"That smoke we saw!" Carol exclaimed. "Could it possibly have been coming from somewhere down here?"

Chris was thinking. "You know, it could at that. If this is a fairly big mine, somebody could have come in from another entrance and could be using it for a camp. It'd be out of the wind, and dry."

"The smoke could have been coming up through a ventilation shaft," Dumont went on. "Hey, I think old Arthur has smelled the bacon, too."

They looked at the big dog. He had trotted ahead of them and he was sniffing the air, too.

Suddenly, they were all reminded of their ravenous hunger.

"How far away do you think the main shaft of this mine might be, Chris?" Dumont said.

"It's hard to say. It might be miles away. Some of these old gold mines have fifty miles or more of tunnels altogether. We're not down to the first level of the mine yet, and there may be more than forty of them."

Dumont walked on ahead. "Well, we're not miles away from that smell," he said. "It draws me like a magnet."

The others followed.

"Hey, what in . . . ?" Dumont suddenly cried in alarm. He reached back and grabbed Chris by the arm.

"Don't move!" he said. "Holy mackerel! I almost did it again!"

"Did what?" Carol asked, stopping behind Chris.

"Look!" Dumont shone his flashlight at a spot in the tunnel floor just ahead of him. There was a hole about five feet square!

"I almost walked right into it," Dumont said. "This falling down holes could get to be a bad habit."

Beyond the hole the tunnel came to a dead end.

Chris got down on his knees and peered down the hole with the aid of his flashlight.

"What is it?" Carol said.

"It's what they call a manway. It leads down to the level below. The ladder looks strong enough." He took hold of the rough wood and tested it.

"You mean that ladder goes all the way down?" Carol asked.

"No, there are a series of landings, about fifteen feet apart. You climb down this ladder to a wooden platform, and then down another ladder to another wooden platform, and so on."

Dumont sniffed hard. "You know, I think that bacon smell is coming up through the manway."

"Must be," Chris agreed. "Opening up that tunnel entrance the way we have would create a draught up this way."

"Well?" Dumont voiced the question that was in all their minds. "Do we go down or back? We can't go any farther in, that's certain."

The other two were silent for a moment, thinking.

"We could go back to the entrance of this tunnel and light a fire, I suppose," Chris said. "Then we could wait until somebody came."

"Who?" Dumont asked. "They're looking for us on the other side of town."

"Maybe not. They may have started looking up this way now. Hey!" he added. "Let's turn on the radio and see if we can find out."

Carol dug into her pocket and brought out the transistor radio. She switched it on. Nothing happened.

"Of course," Chris muttered. "Car radios die out even when you go under an overpass. We won't get a sound down in here. Well, what do you say, Carol? Do we go down? The ladder looks plenty strong."

Carol stared at the hole. "I'm not crazy about the idea," she said. "Still, that smell is sure a powerful persuader."

"Dumont?"

"I'm game. There must be somebody else somewhere in this mine. Bacon doesn't fry itself. And next to food, people are what we need most if we're going to get back home."

"Any people except one," Carol said softly.

The others looked at her. They knew what she meant.

"That's a risk we've got to take," Dumont said. "Come on, let's go."

"Well, okay." Chris drew a deep breath and knelt beside the hole. Arthur came up and began licking his face.

"What about Arthur?" Carol gasped. "He can't climb ladders!"

Chris stood up again. "Yeah, you're right: he can't." Then he came to a sudden decision. "I'm going to try to send him home. Maybe he could bring back help."

"Wonderful!" Carol exclaimed. "I saw a dog on a television show, once. Its master was in trouble, and he just told it to go home and . . ."

"I saw that show, too," Dumont interrupted. "But this isn't television and this," he pointed at the dog, "is Arthur: good, kind, thoughtful, stupid Arthur. Remember?"

"He is not stupid," Chris snapped. He knelt down and put his arm round the big dog's shaggy neck.

"Listen, Arthur. Go and get help, boy. Go and get help!"

Arthur licked his face.

"No, no, you stupid mutt. Home! Go home! He pushed the dog away from him. "Go on now!"

Arthur looked puzzled. He twisted his big head from one side to the other.

Chris pleaded and scolded by turns, and then, wonder of wonders, the big dog got up and trotted back down the tunnel, his tail between his legs.

"Come on." Chris moved over to the hole. "Now's our chance! Quick, before he changes his mind!"

He began to climb down the wooden ladder into the dark shaft. If anything went wrong now, if they were trapped below, they might be trapped forever. They had only a hunch, and a faint smell of bacon to guide them, and even that might lead them into a worse danger than any.

15

The Muffled Man Unwraps

The tough pieces of spruce board had been securely spiked into the two-by-sixes of the ladder. They squeaked under Chris's weight, but they held. When he reached the first board landing he tested it gingerly at first and then put his full weight on it.

"Okay!" he shouted to Dumont and Carol up above. "Solid as a rock. I'm going on down. You follow me."

"Chris!" Carol called. "What about what happened to you on the tower? Does it bother you now?"

"Doesn't seem to. I guess it's because I can't see down. Come on, but don't knock any rock down on my head."

In a few seconds his ski boots were grinding into the rock dust on the next landing. Without waiting for the others, he swung round the ladder and started down the next one. He could hear the others coming behind. Once in a while, a small piece of rock bounced off his head and he realized why miners always wore safety helmets.

The platforms were about twelve feet apart and there were twelve of them altogether. At the bottom, Chris stepped off the ladder into a wider, round-ceilinged cave. It was damp and the floor was littered with rock. He shone his flashlight straight ahead and saw a tunnel curving gently to the right. He guessed that this would be the main tunnel, or drift, as the miners called it, of the first level of the mine.

"How are you making out?" he asked Carol when she came off the ladder, her face and clothes covered with rock dust.

Carol's smile was very thin. "Fine, just fine. But, oh gosh, I would like to sit down for a minute. This girl is bushed!"

"This boy is bushed, too." Dumont stepped off the ladder. He too had picked up a good supply of wet rock on his clothes. "Bushed and hungry." He sniffed hard. "All I can smell now is damp rock, but I did smell bacon back there, I know I did."

Chris looked at the two of them. They had sunk to the floor and were leaning their backs against the rock wall, arms round knees. They were in a bad state, no doubt about it. But it certainly wasn't going to be improved by sitting there.

"Come on," he said. "We've got to get a move on before whoever is in here moves out."

The other two got slowly to their feet. Dumont forced a grin. "One thing you can say for us moles, we don't have to worry about wind and snow."

Chris shone the flashlight along the gloomy tunnel. Its sides and ceiling were of rough, dark-grey rock. Here and there, water dripped from some unknown source.

They had only gone about twenty paces when Carol stopped. "Listen," she said. "I hear something!"

They all stopped and strained their ears. All that they could hear was the steady drip of water somewhere ahead.

"I thought I heard footsteps," Carol said, "but I don't know."

"It was probably just the echo of our own," Chris said. "Come on."

They went on down the curving tunnel until, at last, it forked into two tunnels, like a Y.

"Which one do we take?" Chris said, shining his light down each of them in turn. Both appeared equally gloomy and forbidding.

They sniffed the air anxiously. The bacon smell was there again, but there was no way of telling which tunnel it came from.

"It's like a choice between the Black Hole of Calcutta and the road to the hot place," Dumont said. "Let's go to the right."

"Wait!" Carol had her notebook and pencil out. "I'm going to make a sketch of our route. We may not know where we're going, but at least we'll know where we've been, in case we want to come back.

"Great idea!" Chris said, and shone his flashlight onto the paper, while Carol sketched their route. At the top left-hand corner of the page, she made a small round circle for the hole they had come in through. Then she sketched the long tunnel at the top, the ladders, the main tunnel they had just come along, and now the fork.

Dumont had another idea. "Let's put a marker here. You know, so that if we have to come back this way, we'll know for sure which turning to take."

"Good idea," Chris agreed, putting one stone on top of another in the middle of the passage they were standing in. "Mark that on your drawing, too, Carol."

She nodded and finished off.

Now Chris led the way down the passage to the right. A couple of hundred yards farther on they made another right turn, stopping to let Carol mark it on her sketch. But now the character of the tunnel was changing. Round pine posts, two feet thick, held up a framework of square-cut beams. In some places, where the rock had shifted, the whole framework was leaning over crazily to one side.

"I don't like this at all," Carol said, looking at it uneasily.

"Neither do I." Chris shone his light as far down the corridor as it would go. It looked a little better ahead. "Let's get out of here!"

"Go easy," Dumont warned. "I don't think running down here in these heavy boots is such a good idea. This rock looks as if it's just ready to go. We could easily shake it all loose."

"You're right," Chris agreed. "And a cave-in's about the last thing we want!"

They went on very carefully and now came to an open place where four tunnels met. Chris shone his light ahead down each in turn. "A crossroads," he said.

Then he sniffed. "Boy, that bacon smell is sure strong here!"

At that moment, over against the wall of the tunnel, Carol kicked against something that rattled.

Chris turned the light down to her feet, and what they saw sent their hopes soaring. A frying pan! Carol picked it up. The grease was still warm in it! Chris and Dumont flashed their lights round on the floor: nearby were the remains of a recently extinguished fire and, a little farther along, a knapsack and another bundle.

"The smoke!" Dumont shouted. "This really was where it was coming from!"

"That fire hasn't been out half an hour," Chris said. "Whoever lit it can't be far away."

"And he'll be back," Carol said, "because he's left his things here. Oh dear, now that it's all over I feel like having a quiet cry!"

But Chris had gone over and was shining his light full on the large, khaki-coloured knapsack which lay against the wall. A sudden exclamation from him brought Carol and Dumont over to his side.

The two boys stared at the knapsack as if hypnotized.

"Doodie's!" Dumont exclaimed.

"Sure it is!" Chris breathed. "No doubt about it. I'd know it anywhere. I've seen it often enough hanging on those deer antlers."

They turned their flashlights onto the other bundle. It was a red sleeping-bag. They looked at each other in silence.

"These are the things you said were missing from Doodie's cabin," Carol said nervously.

Chris nodded. No one was willing to be the first to say what that meant.

It was Carol who settled the matter once and for all.

"Look! Over there!" she gasped, as Chris began to play his flashlight round again.

The boys had seen it already. It was a long, soiled piece of white bandage, which had been hastily unwound and dropped on the floor. Near it was a large triangular bandage, knotted into a sling.

16

Trapped Underground

"The muffled man!" Carol gasped. "Those are his bandages. I knew he didn't really need that sling."

"Okay," Dumont said. "Let's get back down that tunnel a bit before we talk, in case he suddenly decides to come back. This changes the look of things."

"But why?" Chris asked, as soon as they were out of sight of the camp area. "Why would he bandage his face and pretend to be hurt if he wasn't?"

"It's a disguise," Dumont said. "Obviously! I don't know why we didn't think of it before, except that I thought that he probably really was injured. He must be someone who knew that his face would be recognized and who put on that bandage to cover it up. He's probably wanted by the police or something!"

"But what about his arm?" Chris objected. "He wouldn't have to disguise that would he?"

"No, but don't you see? That would make the disguise even better. If he just covered up his face, a cop who was looking for him might guess that he was just trying to hide it. But if he bandaged up his arm as well, and put it in a sling, it would take attention away from his face a bit and really make it look as if he had been in a bad accident."

"And another thing," Chris said, frowning. "What could he possibly want here in an old abandoned mine? There can't be any gold left or the mine would never have been closed up. But what else could it be?"

"It could be something he's hidden here and wanted to come back for," Carol suggested.

"The bank robbers!" Dumont shouted. "That's it! It all fits! Doodie, the disguise, the right area, everything!"

"Bank robbers?" Chris exclaimed. "What bank robbers?"

"The ones who robbed the bank at Samo Lake ten years ago!" Dumont said excitedly. "Remember? Chief Greenway said..."

"But they were shot!"

"Not all of them. Two of them were killed and the other one was sent to the penitentiary. And the money has never been found!"

"Say!" Chris's eyes opened wide. "And you think this third guy might have escaped from jail and come back up here to get the money?"

"Could be," Dumont said. "And he'd sure need a disguise if he had escaped from jail, because every cop in the country would be looking for him! We'd better get out of here the same way as we came in," he continued. "Where's your sketch of our route, Carol? I'd rather take our chances out in the bush than be found down here by him!"

But before Carol could get out her notebook, Chris snapped off his flashlight and hissed for silence.

"Listen," he said.

Dumont switched out his light too.

From somewhere not too far away came the unmistakable sound of footsteps.

"Let's get out of here!" Chris whispered, grabbing Carol by the arm and dragging her farther along the tunnel, in pitch darkness.

They hurried down the tunnel, not daring to switch on their flashlights yet, and losing all sense of direction. "This way!" Chris panted at the first turn. They ducked into the side tunnel like rabbits scurrying down a hole, ran a little way, then paused and listened. Not a sound came from any direction.

"I once helped three big guys dig some young foxes out of a hole," Chris said, as if to himself. "I wonder if this is how they felt?"

Nobody answered this. No answer was needed.

And now they had another problem: they had absolutely no idea where they were or which way they should go to get out. In their rush to escape from the muffled man, they had had no chance to look at their map, and now it was useless, unless they went back to the muffled man's campsite and started again from there. But that was an idea that none of them even considered. Chris switched his flashlight on again and shone it back, then ahead. "This tunnel sure curves," he said. "You can't see very far in either direction."

"It keeps going to the right," Dumont whispered. "We'd better take the next tunnel to the left. We don't want to go in a circle!"

But there were no turns to the left. In fact, there were no turns at all. To make matters worse, they had come into another area of loose rock. Here and there, the heavily braced ceilings and walls had given way, dumping piles of rock on the floor. Climbing over these was slow, painful going.

"I wouldn't want to cause any vibrations in here," Dumont said, with a shiver, "or the whole blamed mess might come down on top of us!"

"You think of the most wonderful ideas!" Carol muttered.

Leading the way, Chris said nothing. There had to be another way out of the mine. There just had to be! How had the muffled man got in, for instance? Certainly not by the tunnel they had used. It had been completely covered with snow. They had to find an exit and get out on the lake. Surely somebody would be looking for them in this direction by now!

Then, from back in the tunnel came a new sound, the barking of a dog. Carol and Dumont stopped. Chris, who was twenty feet ahead of them, stopped too.

And then came the second sound: a loud explosion from somewhere quite near, shaking the walls and ceiling violently.

"Look out!" Dumont yelled and, grabbing Carol's arm, pulled her back. Chris started back too, then saw he couldn't make it and turned and ran forwards. The heavy beams collapsed. With a roar, the roof fell in. And, as the air filled with choking clouds of dust, an avalanche of rock and rubble completely blocked the tunnel.

17

Snowscoot Mountie

For a moment Dumont and Carol stood with their eyes closed, shielding their mouths and noses against the dust, numbed by noise, darkness, and terror. Then Dumont opened his eyes and raised his flashlight. At that moment Arthur arrived, barking, from somewhere down the tunnel.

The beam of the flashlight made a funnel through the dust: the tunnel was blocked to the ceiling by chunks of rock and loose debris!

Dumont rushed forwards and began heaving at the pieces of rock, but it was useless. He stopped and stared speechlessly at the rubble.

"Chris! Chris!" Carol called. Her voice echoed in the empty passage. There was no answer. Arthur whined and leaned heavily against Dumont's leg.

The pressure of the dog seemed to shake Dumont out of his inactivity. He reached down and gave the big broad head a slight pat. "Where did you come from, boy?"

"Never mind the dog!" Carol screamed in a panic. "What about Chris?"

"We can't get through there with our bare hands!" Dumont said, pointing at the blocked tunnel. "And we'd better get out of here before more falls down. There must be another way into this mine. Arthur couldn't have climbed down the ladder. He must have gone out and come in by another entrance."

"But Chris . . . ," Carol began.

"He was ahead of the falling rock," Dumont said. "I'm sure of it. The best thing we can do to help him is to get out of here and find help!" Dumont looked down at the dog, and made a quick decision. "Arthur, go home!" he ordered.

"Will he?" Carol asked. "Will he really do it this time?"

"You never know what Arthur will do," Dumont said. "Go home, boy!"

The dog nudged him, almost knocking him off balance.

"No, no, boy. Home! Go home!"

"Please, Arthur," Carol pleaded. "Show us the way out of this horrible place!"

"Maybe if we start, he'll lead the way," Dumont said, walking back down the tunnel. Arthur stood for a moment, looking at the pile of rock that blocked his way forwards, then whined and followed Dumont.

Then, with a quick bark, he bounded ahead.

"Come on, let's follow him," Dumont urged, running behind the dog. Carol followed.

Arthur kept ahead of them, came to a crossroad and took the left turn without any hesitation. Then they came to a fork in the tunnel. Arthur paused for a second to sniff and then took the right-hand branch.

It must be wonderful to have a nose like that, Dumont thought, as he stumbled on after the dog. He was puffing hard. It was becoming more difficult to run, and Carol was getting farther behind.

Then he realized what was happening. They were going uphill. The curving tunnel was rising steeply towards the surface.

"Come on!" he shouted back to Carol. "I think he's taking us out."

Around the next curve they felt a blast of cold air and far ahead saw a small, jagged patch of light.

Thank goodness, Dumont thought, as he stumbled on: somebody's cleared away some of the snow from that entrance. Otherwise we'd never have seen it. Then he realized who it must have been who had cleared away the snow and he didn't feel nearly as good.

They reached the entrance and collapsed in the deep snow. Now, even the freezing wind and blowing snow felt good.

But there was no time for resting. Dumont took stock of their position. The tunnel was one that had obviously been used for hauling things to and from the first level of the mine. It had been blocked up with a sturdy wooden door, but recently somebody had broken through this with an axe. Leading across a small clearing outside, straight towards the entrance to the tunnel, was a set of snowshoe tracks, partly filled in by the new snow.

"Look!" Dumont said eagerly, pointing to the tracks. "He wore snowshoes this far. But he must have taken them off before he went into the mine, so they might be here somewhere." He began looking around for them and, sure enough, finally found them stuck in the space between the top of the door frame and the tunnel roof. Dumont pulled them down. They were brand new.

"These are the ones that were stolen from Dad's store," he said grimly. "I know the make." He laid them side by side on the snow, stepped onto them and, bending over, began to tie them to his feet. Then he leaped out of the entrance.

"Where are you going?" Carol said, trying to keep the fear out of her voice. "Are you going to leave me here?"

"Of course not. I'm going to try to find the place where we first went into this hole. It can't be far from here. Then I'll bring your skis back. It's the only way, Carol. We've got to find help quickly, and we can't travel through the snow on foot. Keep low. I won't be long!" Without looking at her frightened face again, he shuffled quickly across the small clearing, with Arthur bounding along at his side.

Dumont was as good as his word. Carol heard his excited shout and in a few minutes he came shuffling back across the snow, carrying two pairs of skis and poles.

"Here we are," he panted, setting them down beside her. "It's a lucky thing Arthur is with us. It's just about a hundred yards through the bush, but I'd never have found it without him."

They put on their skis.

"Let's go," Dumont said, straightening up.

"Wait," Carol said. "The snowshoes. If we leave them here he'll be able to use them! He might follow us!"

"Good thinking!" Dumont said. He picked up the snowshoes and slung them, trapper fashion, over his shoulder. "He won't get far without these!"

Then he led the way out into the bush. The muffled man's snowshoe trail ran along what looked like a slightly built-up trail through the trees. "I bet I know what this is!" Dumont exclaimed. "It's an old abandoned railway line! They must have used it for hauling out the ore."

"Where do you suppose it leads?" Carol asked.

"I wish I knew. Not to Canot, that's for sure. Canot wasn't even there when this mine was in operation. But let's follow it anyway. It's got to lead somewhere." But, privately, Dumont realized with a sinking feeling that he hadn't the slightest idea whether they were going towards Canot or away from it.

Then he saw something that made him stop dead. "Look!" he shouted, pointing down ahead with his ski pole. "A hydro pole!"

Carol looked and there, down and through the trees, a few hundred yards away, was a gleaming metal standard. But, being a city girl, she didn't realize its significance. "We can't climb that!" she gasped.

"No, but don't you see? There's always a clearing all along the hydro line to protect the wires from the trees. And hydro lines always go somewhere."

Then they heard the noise.

It was away off, and it sounded like a power lawnmower. "What is it?" Carol cried. "A helicopter?"

Dumont listened. "No. I know what it is: a snow scoot!"

"What's that?"

"It's a small thing with skis on the front and a rubber caterpillar belt at the back. It can go over snow like a shot. Trappers use them and forest rangers and . . . hey!"

"What?"

"Hydro workers! That may be one of them now, inspecting the line. Come on. We've got to get down there before he goes past!"

The sound was a steady purr, getting louder all the

time. There was no doubt now that it was travelling along the hydro line.

Dumont dug his poles into the soft snow and pushed hard. They had to get there before that snow scoot passed. It was their only chance. But from the sound of it, they'd never make it. The bush between them and the line was too thick. Then he remembered the snowshoes.

Quickly he bent over, undid his ski harness, and kicked out of it. Within seconds he had transferred his feet from skis to snowshoes. "Wait here!" he shouted to Carol over his shoulder and started through the bush on the dead run.

Dumont was the best boy snowshoer in the district. He had won the junior race at the winter carnival twice. But he never ran faster than he did now.

He could hear the scoot's engine getting louder and louder, and ahead of him and below he could see the line clearing. He came out on a rock ledge twenty feet above it.

Then he saw the scoot, tearing over the snow at at least forty miles an hour, a parka-clad figure hunched over the handlebars behind the plastic windshield.

"Help!" Dumont shouted, stumbling towards the edge of the cliff; but the roar of the tiny motor drowned out his voice.

There was only one thing to do and he did it.

Constable Bert Scott of the Royal Canadian Mounted Police crouched low over the handlebars of his ski scoot and tried to keep most of his face behind the plastic windshield. He could feel his revolver snug against his right hip.

What a day to be out, he thought, let alone lost in the

woods with a possible killer at large! He thought back over the fantastic story that Doodie Horton had told them. But was it possible that those kids could have got away out here, even if that "muffled man" character had? Surely not. There was much more chance of finding them a mile or two away where the snowmobile was searching.

Still, you never knew with kids. It would be just like them to run slap-bang into this muffled guy all the way out here in the bush! Anyway, he had his assignment: to follow the hydro line to a point closest to the lake, scout along the shore, and join up with the snowmobile. They said the boys knew something about woodcraft. They might know enough to follow the hydro line, if they found it, or to stay on the lake shore where they could be seen. And he might always run across some trace of that other one, who had almost scared the wits out of Doodie Horton.

The skis on the front of the scoot slit two narrow tracks in the snow, while the wide rubber tread on the back packed down a neat track.

Funny, he thought as he roared along, how completely empty the bush can seem in winter. Not an animal, not a human being, not even a bird in sight. Then, from somewhere above and to the right, a figure like a snowman in overshoes shot out of the air ahead, landed on the slope and tumbled down directly in his path.

With a grunt of surprise, he jerked the handlebars to the left and barely managed to swerve in time to miss it.

He cut his motor and turned in the saddle, reaching for his gun. There sticking out of the snow was the happiest and at the same time most worried face he'd ever seen.

"Well, I'll be a monkey's uncle!" was all he could say, as he took his hand away from the gun.

"Chris . . . Chris. . . ," the face sputtered. "He's back there in the mine!"

"Mine? What mine?" Constable Scott said. "There's no mine around here."

And then the story began to spill out.

18

Showdown!

At the first sign of the cave-in, Chris had sprung forwards along the tunnel with all his strength and fallen on his face. Stones and dirt piled down on his back, and for one horrible moment he thought he was being buried alive.

Then it stopped.

He lay still, panting and scared. Rock dust filled his mouth and throat. Coughing and spluttering, he lifted his right hand and wiped his face. Then he freed the other arm.

His right leg seemed more cramped than the other. He moved it slowly. Nothing seemed broken. Then, with a cautious heave, he pulled it free and held his breath to see if more rock would fall.

It was pitch dark. Frantically he groped around, bruising his hands against the rock. Then, with enormous relief, he felt the cold metal of the flashlight. Gingerly he pressed down on the switch. The light went on.

For a moment he lay still again. He would have light anyway. Then, remembering the others, he sprang to his feet and shone the light back towards the cave-in. The tunnel was completely blocked. Only a huge, two-foot square beam, held up by two massive posts, was preventing the rest from coming down on him. He knew he should get out of there fast.

But Dumont and Carol! Were they safe or buried? He raised his voice. "Carol! Dumont!"

No answer.

Again he yelled frantically.

Nothing.

Was it because no sound could get through the blocked tunnel, or because Carol and Dumont were past hearing?

The thought was almost too much for him. He stumbled towards the pile of rock and, with his bare hands, tried to heave aside a big jagged piece of it. He couldn't budge it an inch. The tears came to his eyes and he fought them back.

"I've got to get out of here somehow and find help," he muttered. "I've got to!"

He turned and groped his way forwards through the dust of the tunnel, stumbling over loose rock. The light shone dimly ahead of him.

There must be a way out! There must be!

He stumbled on for several hundred yards and then, in the dim, dusty light, saw a blank wall. The tunnel came to a dead end! His heart almost stopped.

But as he came closer to it, he saw that it was really a right-angled turn. His heart jumped with relief as he turned the corner, and then he froze in his tracks. From somewhere ahead, round the next curve of the tunnel, came a gleam of pale yellow light, and the sound of digging. Against the wall of the tunnel, a little way down, leaned a dully gleaming rifle. There was a smell of explosives in the air.

For a moment, Chris stood in the centre of the tunnel,

frozen by surprise and fear. Then he slid back round the tunnel corner and pressed himself against the rock wall, shivering with cold, fatigue, and terror.

So this was where the explosion had come from. The man was trying to uncover something. He remembered the three sticks of dynamite that had been stolen from Dumont's father's store.

And then, as he stood in the dark with his own light out, all he could think of was that this was the end. He was trapped! Behind was the blocked tunnel. Ahead, if they were right about who the muffled man was, was a desperate criminal. There was no other way out.

But gradually, as his panic subsided, he began to think more clearly. There was no reason why the muffled man should come back this way. If he waited until the man had found what he was looking for and went away, he would be quite safe.

But what about Dumont and Carol? He had to get out and try to get help, in case they were trapped or injured. Perhaps there was some way of sneaking past the muffled man. He hadn't looked. He would have to go forward and look round that curve in the tunnel, to see exactly what the situation was.

He switched on his flashlight cautiously and shielded it with his hand as he moved quietly forwards. The sounds of digging still continued.

Chris turned into the curving tunnel and then, his heart beating heavily, slowly moved up to the bend where the rifle leaned against the wall. He looked at it briefly, then squeezed himself flat against the wall as he inched farther along.

As he edged round the corner, he finally saw him: about

twenty feet ahead, digging frantically with a shovel in a small opening. A pick leaned against the wall and, sitting on the floor beside it, an old coal-oil lantern feebly lighted the tunnel.

There was no mistaking him: a tall man, in a ragged sweater, his long black coat flung carelessly on the floor nearby. Chris stared. Now unmuffled, the man's face was clearly visible in the light of the lantern. Running across it at an angle, from cheekbone to neck, was a wide and livid scar, drawn as neatly as if it had been put there with a ruler.

Chris pulled his eyes away and looked at the part of the tunnel the man was working in. There was no way past, except to walk right behind him as he worked, and that was impossible. He was trapped! He would just have to wait.

He squeezed his body back round the corner, hugging the wall closely, and carefully stepping past the rifle again. Then he paused and looked at it.

Did he dare?

Three and a half miles away to the southeast, an aluminum-bodied snowmobile, property of the Canadian army, lumbered along the creek towards Crushed Fly Lake. It was driven by a fur-capped ordnance man, Sergeant Paul Sawalski.

Alec Summerville was also in the cab, and squeezed between him and the sergeant was old Doodie Horton. An open Lands and Forests map of the area covered the two men's knees.

"There she is," Doodie said, pointing a stubby finger at the map. "Right close to Crushed Fly there, about a quarter of a mile from the south of this creek. Most folks think it's a bay of the big lake, but it ain't. That's where my old trapping-cabin was where them robbers made their stand. But that cabin's gone now." His voice was loud over the roar of the engine. "Anyhow, that's where this muffled feller was going to get his bearings. I had to tell him how to find it. He said he could find the other place from there, remembered the way they'd come that day because they'd made a map of it."

"But you didn't tell the boys exactly where the lake was," Alec Summerville said.

"No sir, I sure didn't. But before that, I told them enough so that maybe they could have found her on their own map. The creek'd be a natural way for them to travel. Don't see no tracks of any of them, but of course yesterday's snow and today's wind would have covered all that."

The sergeant reached forwards and took the radio microphone off the hook. "Snowmobile to search headquarters," he called. "Snowmobile to search headquarters. Come in."

The radio crackled. "Okay, snowmobile. This is search headquarters. We hear you. Go ahead."

"We are nearing Crushed Fly Lake on the creek. Concentrating search in this area. Suggest you send all available men this way as soon as they return. That's all." He switched off the set.

"Lots of places they could have spent the night, long as they was okay. They're smart boys. . . ." Doodie began, but his voice died away. He felt very old and very sick.

Then the radio crackled again. "Ski scoot to snowmobile. Ski scoot to snowmobile."

"We read you, ski scoot. Go ahead."

"Have found two children. Boy and girl. Chris Summerville in abandoned mine, near shore of Crushed Fly not far from hydro line. Suspect is also in mine."

The muscles in Alec Summerville's jaw tightened. The short message had sent a shiver of despair through him.

"Know where that is?" he asked Doodie in a voice which he tried to keep steady.

"Never heard of no abandoned mine," Doodie said. "But there could be. This area was pretty active thirty years ago. Our best bet is to get out onto that lake and go up that way."

The sergeant nodded. "Snowmobile to ski scoot," he said. "We will meet you on lake near hydro line." The motor of the snowmobile roared as the accelerator went to the floor. "Use extreme caution. Suspect is armed and dangerous."

The digging inside the tunnel stopped. Chris jerked his hand back quickly from the rifle and stopped breathing. Then he heard some rocks being rolled aside and some muttered cursing. "Hasn't found it yet," Chris thought. He pressed himself against the rock and didn't move a muscle.

Then the digging and puffing and grunting began again, this time more frantically than ever. Again Chris slowly slid his hand down for the rifle. Then he drew back, carrying the rifle with him.

He held it in his hands, breathing hard. What could he do with it now?" If this were a television thriller, he thought, he would walk out and say, "Stick 'em up. I've got you covered." But he knew he couldn't do that. In the first place, he probably wouldn't be able to hit the broad side of a barn with a rifle like this; in the second place, he knew

that he could never even threaten to shoot another human being. But he couldn't let the man have it either.

Then his mind was made up for him. From inside the tunnel came an excited gasp. Then a frantic scraping with the shovel and more cursing, but this time the curses were sounds of satisfaction.

The man had found what he was looking for. Chris made a quick decision.

"There's the ski scoot!" Alec Summerville yelled above the roar of the snowmobile. "See, around that point ahead."

The snowmobile roared across the snow-covered surface of the lake at fifty miles an hour. In a few minutes they were alongside the ski scoot.

"Where are the two children?" Alec Summerville shouted through the open window of the cab.

"Right there on the shore." Constable Scott pointed to the two huddled figures. "Get them inside your cab where it's warm. They showed me the entrance to the mine and I've radio'd Canot for a crew of miners in case there's digging to do. Get your guns and come with me."

In no time Carol and Dumont were safely in the cab of the snowmobile with Doodie, while the three other men, guns in hand, hurried through the bush on snowshoes with Arthur bounding after them.

At the mouth of the mine they stopped. "What do we do now?" Sergeant Sawalski asked. "This might be a mighty big mine. Three of us can't cover it all."

For answer, Alec Summerville called Arthur. The big dog came and stood by his side. Mr Summerville knelt beside him. "Chris always said you were a lot smarter than you look," he said. "Now prove it." He took a length of cord and tied it to the dog's collar. Arthur licked his face.

"Do you think he'll find him?" Sergeant Sawalski asked.

"He's got to find him! Find Chris, boy. Find Chris!" Mr Summerville commanded.

Arthur looked bewildered for a second. Then he barked and dashed into the mine entrance, almost pulling Mr Summerville off his feet.

Chris edged forwards and peered round the corner again as the digging finally stopped. The muffled man was brushing the dirt from a large, square tin box that he had pulled from the rubble. As Chris watched, he pried open the lid and lifted out the contents: packages of money about an inch thick and bound together with paper—thousands and thousands of dollars!

The man knelt on the rock floor and stared at the money. Chris saw his lips moving and then heard him mutter, "At last! Ten years. And this time I keep it."

And then Chris and the muffled man both heard a sound. It came from farther down the tunnel, past the pile of rock where the man had been working. It was the sound of footsteps and the excited whining of a dog.

As the muffled man leapt to his feet, Chris retreated into the darkness. He heard the man close the tin box and pick up the rifle from against the wall, muttering curses under his breath. Then the tunnel went black as the man's lamp went out.

Chris pressed himself back against the wall, waiting, and, in a moment, heard the man's hesitant, shuffling steps as he made his way back down the tunnel in the dark. When the man got close enough, Chris decided, he would have to try to make a dash past him in the dark towards the rescuers. He might run straight into him, or fall and break his neck in the dark, but he would just have to risk that.

The shuffling steps grew close and Chris could hear the man's heavy breathing. He held his own breath. He could hear the sounds of the rescue party more clearly now, and saw the flicker of a light far ahead.

Then he moved, keeping one hand out to avoid running straight into the wall.

There was a sudden, terrific bump, a loud curse, and a pain in his right shoulder. He felt the muffled man's body reel sideways at the unexpected collision. Then he was past, stumbling on towards the faint light, yelling at the top of his voice, and expecting at any moment to be grabbed from behind.

But, within seconds, he was being grabbed instead by his father, while a crazy Arthur tried to leap all over him.

"This man . . . ?" Constable Scott began.

"Back there," Chris said, panting, waving his hand down the tunnel. "He can't get out. It's blocked down there."

"Is he armed?" Sergeant Sawalski said.

Chris nodded, then grinned, reaching into his pocket. "He is, and he isn't. He's got a gun, but I unloaded it. He doesn't know." He displayed the shells in his hand.

"You stay here with the boy," Constable Scott said to Mr Summerville. "We'll deal with him." And, holding their guns at the ready, the two uniformed men moved on down the tunnel.

In five minutes, it was over. The muffled man, trapped by the wall of fallen stone, and with an empty gun in his hands, was quickly overpowered.

Then, after he was led past, Chris sank wearily to the floor, against the rock wall of the tunnel. With a cheerful bark, Arthur licked his face.

Chris put his arms round the big shaggy neck, and leaned against his father's leg. "Good old boy," he murmured. "Who says you're stupid?"

19

Ten Thousand Dollars Reward

"And to think," Carol said, "when I first got a look at Canot out of the train I thought it would be strictly dullsville. How wrong can a city gal be?"

It was the night following the rescue. The three adventurers were sitting on the rug in front of the living-room fire. They'd been there all evening. In fact, they felt they might just never leave that fire.

Mrs Summerville hovered over them like a mother dog over her pups, keeping them well supplied with hot chocolate. She smiled a lot and frowned, too, and often was close to tears. Now and then she would reach down and lay her hand on one of their heads for no apparent reason.

Chris had his stocking-clad feet propped up on a chair. He was sipping his chocolate. "Dullsville," he grunted. "We try to make it interesting. Of course getting lost was a little extra. In fact, it was pretty blamed stupid," he added disgustedly.

"And we can't always guarantee an abandoned mine and a cave-in and a desperate criminal," Dumont added. He was lying with his head and shoulders resting on Arthur, who obviously didn't mind because he was sound asleep.

"You can't take credit for the muffled man," Carol said, with a little shiver. "I brought that bird with me."

Chris sat up straight. "You know, I still can't figure out why he bothered to disguise himself like that if he wasn't wanted by the police. You know, we thought he must have broken out of jail, but he hadn't. He'd been released a few months ago."

"That's easy," Dumont said. "There are lots of people up here who remember that robbery and who might recognize him. Chief Greenway, for instance. He was a cop in Samo Lake then. Besides, the police always keep a watch on released prisoners when they think they might go back for some loot they hid before they went to jail. He really needed that bandaged face, and the arm in the sling was to make it more genuine, the way I said."

Mr Summerville came in then. He still looked tired and worn. "Well, they shipped your muffled man back to the city," he said, hanging up his heavy coat and sinking into a chair. "He'll have to face another charge of robbery, apart from anything else. He certainly seems to have been the one who broke into the stores. It's lucky for him that it's not going to be a murder charge. He can thank Chris for that, for unloading his rifle. There's no doubt he would have used it, the way he did ten years ago to resist arrest. And in that mine he could hardly have missed."

"I still don't understand why you unloaded that rifle," Dumont said seriously. "Why didn't you keep it and, well, I mean, you could have . . ."

"Could have what?" Chris asked. "Shot the man with it? Could you?"

"Me?" Dumont cried. "You know me. I can't even shoot a rabbit."

"That's what I mean. It's easy to watch it on television, but when you've got a gun in your hand it's different. And if I'd kept the gun or hidden it, he'd have known I was there and come looking for me." Chris shuddered. "And if nobody had turned up to look for me right then, he'd have found me, too!"

"Yeah." Dumont shook his head thoughtfully. "I see what you mean. I wonder why he had to blow up part of the mine to find his loot."

"It was sealed in," Mr Summerville said. "I got the whole story clear at last from Chief Greenway this afternoon. Some of it even he didn't know until this muffled man of yours spilled the beans last night. When these three bandits blew the vault of the Samo Lake bank ten years ago, they got a great deal more money than they'd expected: all the mine payrolls.

"When they found the road south blocked ahead of them, they headed up into the bush. It was summer. They stole a canoe and crossed a stretch of Crushed Fly Lake, to throw the police trackers off their trail, and then headed into the bush again. They stumbled on this old mine just the way you did and decided to hide most of the money there and come back for it later, when the hunt had died down. They had more than they could carry comfortably and knew that they could never get through any police road-blocks with it."

"And they sealed it in?" Carol said.

"Yep. Your muffled man was the expert safe-cracker. He still had some explosives with him, so they put the money in a small side tunnel in a big tin toolbox they'd taken out of their car and blew the walls down on it, so that no one else would be able to find it. When he went back for it this time, he knew he'd need some explosives to shift some of the rock."

"That mine was made to order for a hiding-place," Dumont said. "Why didn't the bank robbers stay in there themselves?"

"They did for a while, but they had no food, no water, no warm clothing, nothing to make a fire with: no equipment of any kind. They'd set out to rob a bank, not camp out in the bush, so they weren't prepared. What they had to do was break out of the police net and get back down south. But they'd only got a few miles from the mine when the police spotted them again from a search plane. That's when they came across Doodie's old cabin and holed up there."

"Then Doodie didn't know where they'd left the money, after all?" Chris said. "Good old Doodie! I knew he couldn't have been mixed up with those guys. He's no crook."

"All Doodie knew," Mr Summerville went on, "was that these three men suddenly burst in on him in his old trapping-cabin, held him prisoner, and then started a gun battle with the police. He dived under his bunk and stayed there until it was all over: until two of them were dead and this third one was unconscious from that terrible bullet wound in his face and neck."

There was a knock on the front door. Mr Summerville stopped talking to go and open it. It was Gratien LePage.

"Name of a name," he said, scowling, and rubbing his hands together. "That wind is blowing worse than ever. Good thing you kids aren't out in that." He scowled heavily again at the three youngsters and shook his head. "I just can't get used to the idea that two boys who've lived here all their lives could be foolish enough to go out like that into strange bush. Don't you ever go into the bush again without telling us exactly where you're going."

"Don't worry, Dad, we won't!" Dumont assured him.

"And your friend, Doodie Horton," Mr LePage went on, flashing a quick grin. "What a one that is. He says he wants to see you: something about a special bait."

"Good old Doodie," Chris said. "He sure has had a bad time." He paused and frowned. "Say, you know another thing I've never understood? Why did the muffled man go and see Doodie anyway, when he came into town? I should have thought that he'd stay away from anyone who was likely to know who he was, not go and announce that he was back like that."

"Ah, but he had to go and see Doodie," Mr Summerville said, "because only Doodie could tell him how to find the money!"

"But you just said that Doodie didn't know where the money was, Dad!" Chris exclaimed.

Mr Summerville smiled. "He didn't. But what he did know was where his old cabin was, or rather, where it had been. The muffled man needed to know that to find the mine. The bandits knew pretty clearly how they had got from the mine to Doodie's cabin..."

"That's what was on the map he dropped in the train," Carol said.

"Yes. The muffled man could find his way from Doodie's cabin, or the spot where it had been, to the mine," Mr Summerville went on. "But he had no idea how to get to Doodie's cabin to begin with. He was unconscious when they carried him out of there after the gun fight, and all he knew was that it had been somewhere north of the town of Canot. He learned that much at the trial, as well as exactly who Doodie was, because Doodie had to appear and give evidence against him."

"So when he got here, the first thing he did was go and see old Doodie!" Dumont exclaimed. "And threaten to kill him if he didn't tell him the location of his cabin, and if he told the police about it afterwards!"

"Yes, that's true," Gratien LePage said. "He was just telling me about this again. Ha, he is really shaken up, that one! This muffled man came to his cabin, forced his way in, and threatened to kill him if he didn't give him the information he wanted, or if he told the police. Then he made Doodie tell him what things he would need to camp up in the bush and went out again to steal them—from my store, *parbleu*! Then he came back again and slept in Doodie's cabin, right across the doorway, so that no one could get in and Doodie couldn't get out, and the next day he started out, taking some extra things of Doodie's with him: his knapsack and a sleeping-bag. The nerve of that one! On a pair of my best snowshoes!"

"But how could he find Doodie so easily as soon as he came into town?" Chris objected. "He's not in the phone book."

"No," Mr Summerville said. "Chief Greenway checked into Doodie's story, too. It seems this man phoned the operator and asked for Mr Doodie Horton. Well, she knows Doodie as well as most folks round here do and so she said he didn't have a phone. But she told the man how to find his cabin!"

"That's one advantage of living in a small town," Dumont said, with a grin at Carol. "Everyone can always direct gangsters to where you live!"

"Then the muffled man was phoning when I saw him in the phone booth at the station!" Carol said. "I thought he was talking to someone!"

"Any more questions?" Mr Summerville said, with a laugh.

"Yes," his wife said, getting up from her chair. "How about bed for these three young crime-busters? They've had enough excitement again for today."

But before anyone could make a move, there was another knock at the front door.

This time it was Chief Greenway. He politely refused Mrs Summerville's invitation to come in and sit down, but stood beside the hall door, straight as a baseball bat, his cap in his hands.

"You kids have caused a lot of people a lot of trouble," he said.

There wasn't any answer anybody could make to this.

"You've worried your parents, and you've had half the country out. It's just a lucky thing that nobody else got lost while they were beating around in the bush. You don't seem to realize that people risked their lives searching for you. That's the trouble with kids nowadays. . . ."

"Just a minute, Chief," Alec Summerville interrupted. "You're perfectly right when you say they've caused a great deal of trouble. But I can't agree that they don't realize what they've done. They realize it only too well."

"We sure do," Chris spoke up, and the others nodded their agreement.

"They didn't plan to get lost, that's for sure," Gratien LePage added. "It was an accident. Sure they made some pretty stupid mistakes. But we all make them, eh? Besides," he added, "if it wasn't for these kids, they never would have caught that bank robber and got back all the money, no?"

Chief Greenway looked very pained. He'd been going to say this very thing himself, after he'd got round to it. But first, he figured, it was his duty to read the kids a good stiff lecture. They could always use it. Now LePage had spoiled his speech.

"I was coming to that," he said stiffly. "And I've had a wire from the headquarters of the bank. There was a reward of ten thousand dollars posted for the recovery of that money. It still stands."

Chris let out a whoop that could be heard at the end of the block. Dumont did a somersault on the middle of the rug. Carol clapped her hands with delight.

"Wait a minute," Chris said suddenly. "Old Doodie's entitled to some of that. After all, he was the one who got us found."

The others agreed.

Mrs Summerville was laughing at their antics. "Goodness, I'm afraid nobody's going to be the least interested in Christmas around here now!" She smiled.

"Christmas!" Carol shouted. "Oh yes, indeed! Won't we be able to buy some Christmas presents now!"

And then her face became serious. "You know, it'll soon be over. It's going to feel kind of funny going back to the city at the end of holidays: funny and dull. I hope you'll invite me up again."

"Of course we will," her aunt said. "But I should think you'd never want to see the town of Canot again!"

"Just try me, Aunt Mary, just try me," her niece laughed. "Just try me and see!"

Dumont grinned. "Sure, and just to make certain that you'll want to come back, tomorrow we'll take you ice-fishing."

"Oh no!" Carol said, pretending to tear her hair. "Oh no! Not again!"

THE SECRET CIRCLE

1. THE MYSTERY OF MONSTER LAKE / David Gammon
2. THE RIDDLE OF THE HAUNTED RIVER / Lawrence Earl
3. THE LEGEND OF THE DEVIL'S LODE / Robert Collins
4. THE SECRET TUNNEL TREASURE / Arthur Hammond
5. THE MYSTERY OF THE MUFFLED MAN / Max Braithwaite
6. THE CLUE OF THE DEAD DUCK / Scott Young

General Editor ARTHUR HAMMOND